A missile passed by the port side of Crackers's Apache. Their mission was to keep all armor and antiair out of action while Bad Bear and Horwitz took out all defenses around the missile.

Three tanks, dug in with their guns pointing skyward in an antiaircraft mode, fired their main guns and machine guns at the Apache. A 76.2 mm round from a T-76 hit the helicopter in the right side and nearly spun it out of control.

Crackers was slammed to one side of the cockpit when the round hit. He fought to regain control as wind blew through the gaping hole in the helicopter . . .

SPECIAL PREVIEW!

Turn to the back of this book for a special excerpt from an exciting new military series . . .

AIRBORNE

. . . an epic saga in the bestselling tradition of W.E.B. Griffin's *Brotherhood of War*.

The Eagle Attack Team Series by Larry Hicks

EAGLE ATTACK TEAM
FORCE RED

LARRY HICKS

DIAMOND BOOKS, NEW YORK

This book is a Diamond original edition, and has never been previously published.

FORCE RED

A Diamond Book / published by arrangement with the author

PRINTING HISTORY
Diamond edition / January 1993

ISBN: 1-55773-847-5

Diamond Books are published by The Berkley Publishing Group,
200 Madison Avenue, New York, New York 10016.
The name "DIAMOND" and its logo are trademarks
belonging to Charter Communications, Inc.

PRINTED IN THE UNITED STATES OF AMERICA

10 9 8 7 6 5 4 3 2 1

Dedicated to my children,
David, Jr., Sandra, Daniel, & Ty,
army brats, all.

In Memory of those lost souls who kept up the fight against Communism.

MEMBERS OF
EAGLE ATTACK TEAM

Lieutenant Colonel Mack "Truck" Grundy, U.S. Army, Retired, Korean War and Vietnam War vet, infantry, paratrooper, Special Forces, helicopter and fixed-wing qualified, Texas cowboy turned soldier.

Chief Warrant Officer Cliff "Bad Bear" Sate-Zalebay, U.S. Army, Retired, Vietnam War vet, Special Forces, parachute, helicopter qualified, demolition expert, Kiowa Indian.

Lieutenant Colonel Stewart "Stu" Barringer, U.S. Army, Retired, Korean War and Vietnam War vet, Special Forces, qualified in many special project areas, an expert in operations, member of a number of POW raids in Laos and North Vietnam.

Lieutenant Johnny "Crackers" Grahame, U.S. Navy, Retired for minor medical disability, helicopter qualified, test pilot, not a war veteran and tries to make up for it.

Lieutenant Colonel Matty "Red Dog" Bavaros, U.S. Air Force, Vietnam Veteran and Air Force Commando in Laos, helicopter and fixed-wing rated, angry at the world, eats raw steaks washed down with Scotch, too mean to work with regular air force people.

Captain Amal "Turk" Turki, U.S. Army, in Panama invasion, expert gunner and computer specialist in the Apache.

Command Sergeant Major William "Willie" Falloure, U.S. Army, Retired, Special Forces and paratrooper qualified, Vietnam War veteran, covert assignment in Laos with code name of "Black Panther," expert working with indigenous personnel in counter-guerrilla, married to a Filipino woman.

Lieutenant Colonel Donald "Bo Peep" Day, U.S. Air Force, Retired, Vietnam War and Laos veteran, flew observation planes with Raven Project in Laos, multi-engine qualified, old "Asian hand" married to Thai woman many years before her death.

Warrant Officer Wallace "Wally" Burnham, U.S. Army, Vietnam War, copilot on UH-1.

Captain Tyron "Clench" Riggs, U.S. Army, flew Apaches in the Panama invasion.

Warrant Officer Amos "Pieface" Pylant, U.S. Army, gunnery expert in Apache.

Warrant Officer Arturo "Spic" Velasco, U.S. Marine Corps, gunnery expert in Apache.

Warrant Officer Edward "The Fly" Horwitz, U.S. Army, gunnery expert in Apache.

Major William "Wild Bill" Flanagan, U.S. Army, aviator.

Captain Tomas "Flaco" Hernandez, U.S. Air Force, gunnery expert in Apache.

Warrant Officer Roger "Full Drive" Miller, U.S. Army, aviator.

Warrant Officer Elroy "Buddy" McGee, U.S. Navy, gunnery expert in Apache.

Warrant Officer 1st Class Jackson "Push" Okahara, U.S. Army, AH-64 helicopter maintenance specialist, veteran of Panama invasion, and a first class physical specimen who got his nickname "Push" because he could drop and do over 200 pushups at any time.

Sergeant First Class (E-7) George ''Nickel'' Seybold, U.S. Army, SOCOM, AH-64 helicopter maintenance, veteran of the Vietnam War, ranger and airborne qualified, expert armorer of the AH-64.

Sergeant (E-5) Martin ''Jar'' Peek, U.S. Marines, SOCOM, AH-64 maintenance specialist, yearns to be a pilot and paratrooper.

Warrant Officer Stanton ''Belch'' Fullove, U.S. Army, computer and electronic expert.

EAGLE ATTACK TEAM
FORCE RED

1

Tech reps from various companies studied the after-action reports that members of the Eagle Attack Team had written up on the AH-64 Apache helicopter after their return from Saudi Arabia. The Apache helicopter performed beyond its expectations during Operation Desert Storm, as far as the Apache program detractors were concerned. The same helicopters, however, had performed exactly as designed, as far as the builders and supporters of the program were concerned. After their stellar performance in Desert Storm, the war birds were now a permanent part of the U.S. military arsenal.

Warrant Officer Jackson Okahara, U.S. Army, chief maintenance officer for the team, babied his six charges as if he were the only person able to properly maintain them. The maintenance and helicopter crew members smiled as the young warrant officer fussed over every detail. They knew that it was his expertise that kept their six helicopters at such a high level of readiness.

Lieutenant Colonel Mack "Truck" Grundy, U.S. Army, Retired, commander of the highly classified team, watched the busy men in the hangar. This mixed bag of pilots and support members from all the services had performed like the professionals they were. And this team was a mixed bag in every respect. He had retired and active duty members from all of the military services. The men were of officer, warrant officer and enlisted ranks. Within the two-year period since the activation of the team, they had been on five missions in five different parts of the world. They had won out over the enemy in every situation. They had been so successful that many of the men took it for granted that they could not be stopped by anyone.

Chief Warrant Officer Cliff "Bad Bear" Sate-Zalebay, U.S. Army, Retired, walked up beside Truck. He growled with pleasure as he looked over the men before them, "Those guys are good, boss. Damned good."

"I'll agree with that," replied Truck.

"Now that the Soviets are breaking up and we don't got the terrible Red Bear to fight no more, what's gonna become of us warriors, Truck?" asked Bad Bear.

Truck looked at the tall Kiowa Indian and smiled. He and Bad Bear had been on tours in Laos and Vietnam together while on active duty, and now they were glad to be reunited on this special team. They had many battles under their belts. Truck told him, "Where there's people, there's gonna be trouble."

"I don't know if it'll ever be the same for us Regular Army men, Truck. You was in the Korean War, the Vietnam War and on a lot of operations in other parts of the world. You've had a good life of following the warrior's path. I got in on some of it, but I'd sure hate to be a young soldier in this day and age, not knowing if I was ever gonna go to war or not. What a boring way to face the future."

"Don't rule out the Russians or their old allies causing trouble," Truck said. "A dictator'll show up before it's done. When things get bad, and they're already bad, a strong arm will show up and take charge. They don't know a thing about democracy, and it'll take some time for them to get things straightened out—if ever. Look at their leaders now. They're preaching reform and democracy, but they want to keep all the power for themselves and not share it."

"Hell, that sounds like the Congressmen of the U.S. of A., boss," quipped Bad Bear. "They ain't gonna let nobody in to take their place."

"Can't blame 'em with that big retirement they're gonna get from us taxpayers when they do retire," Truck reminded him. "So, let's say politicians are alike all over the world. Now ain't that a cause for worry?"

Bad Bear grinned at the one-eyed man with the black leather patch over his left eye. He agreed, saying, "Reckon you're right, boss."

Truck looked over the working men and the black-painted war machines with satisfaction. He told Bad Bear, "The men did good, damned good, in Desert Storm. In fact, the men do good every time they've been called upon."

"Yep, but it's another time we won't get credit for our work," commented Bad Bear. "And I agree that they're a bunch of good men."

"Why don't ya go up to Oklahoma and see your folks?" asked Truck.

"As soon as these birds and all related equipment is in STRAC condition."

Truck knew that would be Bad Bear's response, but he wanted his old friend to know that he should go home and see the old folks. A man in this business never knew when it would be his last visit home.

Crackers Grahame appeared at the door of the office. He called to Truck, "Dot's on the phone, Truck!"

"Which one?" asked Truck.

"Your ex."

"Oh, hell," Truck said under his breath. He walked back to the office and to his desk. He picked up the phone and asked, "What do ya need, Dot?"

"Damn! You make me so mad. You're so direct, to the point," she complained. Then she tried to tone down the anger in her voice and said, "I'm a little short this month, Truck."

Yeah. Brains, thought Truck, then he asked, "Short of what, Dot?"

"Funds. You know, money."

"When are you not short?" asked Truck bluntly.

"I know you don't owe me anything, Truck. I've been married enough times since you and I broke up, but you're the only one I can ever turn to."

"What about the money your dad left you? Where's all of that?"

"I can't touch any of it. The old codger put it in a trust, and I get it doled out to me once a month," she said.

"The old man was smarter than both you and your mother put together," he said in a matter-of-fact voice. Then he asked, "Okay, what's the problem?"

"I've got to pay on my house and my car. I'm a month behind on both of them."

"Dot, I'll give you the money—this time. But I want it paid back on the first of the month. If you don't pay it back, I'm gonna tell you to go to hell next time."

"But that'll leave me with nothing to spend the rest of the month," she complained.

"Like hell. You'll still have a couple of thousand dollars after you pay all your bills. That oughta be enough for anyone, especially when that person freeloads off all the men she can shack up with.''

"Truck, you're too mean to me sometimes. I know I didn't treat you right when we were married, but I'm not all that bad.'' There was self-pity in her voice.

"You're all that bad, Dot. I'm just a sucker because you happen to have been my first wife, and I think I still owe ya something. But that was a long time ago, so don't keep riding it.''

"Okay, Truck.''

From the clipped words and tone of her voice, Truck knew that she was about to explode. But she knew that if she started on him, he'd hang up the phone and wouldn't talk to her for months. She needed his largess at the moment.

"Come by the club for lunch and I'll have the money,'' he told her.

"Thank you, Truck,'' she said, a pout in her voice. After a pause, she told him, "No matter what I say or how I blow off, you're a good man, Truck.''

"Goodbye, Dot.'' Truck put down the phone. He looked over at Crackers, who was doing his best to ignore hearing the conversation. Truck said, "I'm going to the bank in a short while and then to the club for lunch.''

"Gotcha, boss.'' The retired navy lieutenant watched Truck as he left the office. He smiled. Dot was lucky Truck was the kind of person he was. Crackers knew Dot to be one hell of a bitch.

Truck walked out into the hangar where Warrant Officers Okahara and Fullove stood waiting for him. They were as dirty and greasy from hands-on work as the maintenance men who worked for them. "Whatcha got, boys?''

"That army procurement officer from Saint Louis is gonna be here this afternoon,'' Okahara reminded him.

"He's got a few new goodies for us to try out on these Apaches."

"He's got some new electronics, as well as new sighting devices," put in Fullove.

"I'll be here," Truck informed them.

Truck walked around the huge hangar, talking to the men and observing their work. The young soldiers were very respectful when in the presence of this legend and felt it was a great honor to be in his command. Not only did he know his business as a commander, he thought winning was doing battle with as few losses to his command as victory would allow.

Red Dog Bavaros looked up but didn't smile when Truck walked by. The old air force lieutenant colonel admired Truck himself, but it just wasn't the nature of the red-faced man to act over friendly to anyone.

"Red."

"Truck."

Truck had a hidden smile as he passed the old aviator. Red Dog was among the best Apache helicopter pilots Truck had seen. He was glad to have him aboard, even if he was a sour-faced, mean-dispositioned old codger. Truck never worried about the personalities of his men, only what they could do on the job.

He looked at his watch and left early to make a visit to the bank.

Colonel Ralph Betts, army procurement officer for the AH-64 Apache helicopter arrived. Betts had been instrumental in the success of the helicopter. He demanded the best and wouldn't let the vendor companies take short cuts in designing and building the helicopter. A two-tour combat chopper jockey in Vietnam, he understood the importance of high survivability in an aircraft fighting a war. He, along with thousands of other aviators, swore a number of times in Vietnam that if he ever had a chance to assist the army in getting a new helicopter, he would make sure it met all the demands of the army chopper pilot. He had done a great job.

"I saw your daughter, Linn, in Saudi Arabia, Truck," Betts told Truck. "She was doing fine and having the time of her life flying support over troubled waters, so to speak. She's a chip off the old block, that's for sure."

"Most say she's the better part of that block," chuckled Truck. There was a strong note of pride in his voice.

"This new equipment I've got, Truck, is the best and is still classified. It's so highly classified that it doesn't even exist," Betts told him. "We've got a new target acquisition system that will home in on anything that is radioactive. It's so selective that it'll bypass any radioactive signals occurring in nature. It knows the signals of all manmade nuclear devices. It should knock nuclear missiles out of the air with no problem. It'll do that by hitting the missile in the body and not in the warhead, thereby not causing a nuclear explosion."

Truck raised his eyebrows at that.

"Plus it's got a new computer system that will be up to date far into the future," continued Betts. "And it weighs only sixty-four pounds. We were able to get rid of enough other equipment to more than balance out this new system."

"Damn! I can hardly wait to see it work," said Truck.

"Have fun. We did, building and testing it," said Betts.

Truck agreed he would.

After looking around, Betts told him, "I'm glad you finally got rid of that old Huey and got a Blackhawk."

"That old Huey was a damned good chopper," said Truck.

"Agreed. But old it was. It was as outdated as some of

the soldiers I know in this army. You needed an update, and with the Blackhawk, ya got it.''

"Ya stayin' for the night?'' asked Truck.

"I wish I could, but I've got to get back,'' said Betts. "I'd like to spend the evening getting loaded with a bunch of chopper jocks. I miss that more than anything, this being up in some damned office away from the troops.''

"We in the chopper-driving business are glad you're there,'' Truck assured him. It was a compliment.

Betts introduced Truck to the men who would place the new equipment in the aircraft. The Blackhawk would be updated to be compatible with the Apaches. After a cup of coffee and a few war stories, Betts left and went back to Saint Louis.

Truck called LTC Stu Barringer, U.S. Army, Retired, the team's operations officer, into the office. "Let's get a training program set up for these new playthings we're getting. We've gotta keep up to snuff no matter what the Reds are doing.''

"Agreed. I'll get right on it,'' he said and left to do his business.

Professionals trained and played for real no matter what the world situation was at a given time. Properly trained men had a better chance of survival when the balloon went up. Truck and his men were professionals.

2

The wind blew snow in swirls around Stan Styczyski as he stepped from the Kremlin to his waiting sedan. He was thankful that the new Russian Government recognized his Soviet passport and visa for travel to the United States. Trouble was brewing for the people and republics of the old Soviet Union, and he didn't want to be there when things really fell apart. Old ethnic hostilities and a non-existant economy in the new republics were causing many conflicts within the new Commonwealth. With leaders refusing to give up power and go the democratic route, more and more countries were going the way of Georgia. Some elected democratic leaders were like the leaders of Ukraine and didn't want to relinquish leadership of their armies. A strong leader must appear in this new Commonwealth of nations if things were going to be held together. He saw no strong leader coming forth in the near future. They all wanted to hold on to the power they had amassed before the crumbling of the Soviet Union. Once a Communist always a Communist, as far as Stan was concerned.

Avel, the chauffeur of his car, held the door open against the strong wind. Stan got into the back seat. The car was one of the perks Soviet officials, as well as the new republic officials, refused to give up willingly. The automobile with driver was a visual sign to the masses that you had made it in the Party. A person riding in the back seat of a sedan was not considered a "common man" in this classless society, but one of the exalted bureaucratic leaders. Exalted was a strong word for the most badly managed, incompetent bureaucracy that the world had ever known.

God! thought Stan. How could such a corrupt, inefficient system have lasted so long? It had always been one of the great mysteries of life to him.

Avel got into the car and pulled out into an empty Red Square. The headlights of the car had trouble piercing the heavy snowfall. This storm was the last gasp of winter, and it was doing its best to outdo the winter storms of the past few weeks.

"So, you leave us and go to America, eh, Comrade?" asked Avel.

"Yes. You know my family has been there since the end of the Great War," said Stan.

"Aye, so I know," the driver admitted. "I wish I had a family in America to go to."

"Take a chance and go anyway," suggested Stan.

"No, I have too much family and responsibilities to go off like a young man on an adventure," stated Avel, then turned back to his business.

Stan knew the man would never take a chance and venture alone into such an unknown change in his lifestyle. Avel was a product of a failed political experiment called Communism. He had been taken care of from his cradle, and he wanted the state to take care of him to his coffin—a life with all needs met from birth to death. A future without the state being his "Big Father" scared him.

Stan Styczyski was Polish by birth and had spent only a few months of his life in the United States after World War II. During World War II, he left Poland and joined the Russians to fight against the Nazis. He had fought well and had risen in the officer corps of the Soviet Army.

He knew the brutality of the Russians well and had warned his parents to flee Poland before they arrived. His father, mother and some of the family had escaped by ship hours before the Russians arrived to liberate their town.

When the war ended, Stan had received permission from his commanding general, an old ex-Tsarist professional soldier who had embraced Communism and joined the Red Army, to leave the army and join his parents. The surprise of his life came when he received an order personally signed by the general releasing him and giving him safe passage through the lines to the British sector. He went to join his family in the Polish ghetto of Cleveland, Ohio. There he met John Sikorski, a Pole from the old country, who had been a member of the American O.S.S. during the war. John enlisted Stan into becoming a mole in the Soviet Army for the U.S. Stan returned to Russia and rejoined the Red Army. He had to give up his wartime rank of colonel and become a peacetime captain. Later he was asked to leave active duty and work as a civilian with the People's Commissar for Defense. He remained in the army reserves and attained the rank of colonel.

He was assigned to military personnel and became a *nomenklatura*. He was never able to penetrate any Soviet intelligence agency. But in his position, he gave the U.S. Central Intelligence Agency valuable information on the size of the Soviet military, where elite and technical personnel were assigned, and information about special units and their locations.

Stan's Ukrainian wife was willing to leave the failing Soviet Union and start a new life in the United States. He informed her that at the age of sixty-eight, he did not have much to offer his new country. She felt being in America was worth it no matter what sacrifices they had to make. He was also working on the process of getting their children to the United States. Maybe his case officer, who had been John Sikorski the entire time, would have some pull in expediting the process.

He was not going back to America empty handed. He had valuable information about Soviet civilian and military leaders who were forming a new military-oriented region to challenge the rest of the republics of the former Soviet Union. These civilian and military bureaucrats feared their loss of power and the privileges their positions gave them. They were not going to give up their power gracefully.

Avel stopped at the front door of Stan's house and got out to open the rear door.

Stan stopped and said, "I will be leaving in a few days. I hope you get someone who is easier to chauffeur than I have have been over the years."

"It has been a pleasure to drive you, Comrade Poland," Avel smiled. Avel was one of the few persons who had not resented the Pole's rise to power over the years. "You have been an army officer and worked in the military for many years, eh?"

"Since Nineteen and Forty-one. I was eighteen years old. That is a long time, but they still would not let me retire until now," complained Stan.

"You too good a man," laughed Avel. "See, too good of a man always gets tied deep to the Party and they use him up until he is a dried up old man. Then there is no time left to enjoy your retirement.''

"That is the way life is," said Stan in a tired voice.

"Goodbye, Poland," said Avel in farewell.

Stan shook his hand and went into the building.

Yelena had opened the door to their apartment for him when she heard the car drive up. She offered a round, chubby cheek for him to kiss as he entered. She had been such a pretty, trim thing when they were married forty years before. Harsh Russian winters and too much starchy food had taken its toll on her.

"We have food?" asked Stan.

"I stand in the line for three hours for one small roll of sausage. We don't have much food, Stan. We must go to America soon or your fat little Yelena will grow skinny and you will freeze to death next winter," she laughed. It is better to laugh than to cry in such circumstances.

"All we need is enough food for a few days more," he told her, taking his heavy coat off and hanging it in the closet near the door. Because of the lack of heat, he left his light coat on. It was so cold in the house that fog escaped their mouths with every breath and every word.

The need for food and the lack of food had become paramount during the winter. He and Yelena had hoarded as much food as they could get their hands on, but they had given most of it to their children and grandchildren.

Stan walked down the corridor of the neat apartment and used the single bathroom. Because of his position, he had a three bedroom apartment not far from the Kremlin. But there was no position powerful enough to get food that was not available in Moscow, unless a person was a very high official or he was plugged in to the black market. He was glad that his daughter had gone to stay with Yelena's parents in the country in Ukraine. They had more food than the large cities.

He stopped outside his son's door for a moment before knocking and pushing it open. His thirty-three-year-old son, Viktor, lay on the bed, an empty bottle on the floor beside his bed. His son was one of the many alcoholics in the Soviet Union. He had no job, no hope for a job and had become such a spaced-out boozer that he didn't care if he ever found a job. Viktor had become crazed when he learned that his parents were going to America and leaving him behind. He had been gone for three days and nights before he was found sleeping in an alley. Toes of his left foot had frozen and three had been amputated at the hospital.

Stan closed the door and joined his wife in the kitchen, the warmest part of the house.

"We must go soon, my husband, before we are all dead," stated Yelena, not turning from the stove.

"Yes, that is true," agreed Stan. He walked to the window and looked out. A signal on the corner lamppost beckoned him to meet an agent he worked with. He would go. He had been too long in the business not to go and learn new information. "I will go out for a while. I have much to think about."

"Yes, I'm sure. You are leaving behind your old friends and about to venture into a new world," said Yelena. "Supper, what there will be of it, will be ready in two hours. That will give you time to meet and drink with our friends."

Without another word, Stan left for his appointed meeting.

Stan found Aleksandr at the bar they frequented. Aleks had already bought vodka and spent his last rubles to purchase a few hard, sourdough-type crackers for them to munch on.

Aleks greeted Stan with a wry smile and announced, "If the new government cannot find more money, this is the last of my food. If I can last until summer, I'm going into the countryside and start farming."

"Go to Ukraine," advised Stan. "My wife has family there who will help you."

Aleks nodded his thanks and at the same time passed Stan a piece of paper. Without looking at it, Stan secretly placed it in his pocket.

Aleks went on, "This new government, huh. They are all crooks, like the last. The only difference is that this one was elected. But a thief is a thief no matter who put him in power."

"I don't trust this new bunch, either. In fact, are they not the same ones who were once Marxist Communist, die-hard members of the Red Party, who believed in the system?" asked Stan, voicing his lack of trust in the new heads of government. "Will they not get a taste of power and wish to hold onto it even after the people vote them out and want them to step down?"

Both men grumbled in their glasses and munched on the hard crackers. At least they could speak of their dissatisfaction in this new "democracy." Two years before and they would have been hauled off to the infamous Lubyanka prison for voicing such anger toward the ruling Red Party members.

After much talk and drinking cheap vodka, and without much visible show of parting, Stan took his leave and started walking the three blocks back to his home. The snow was still falling, but the wind had died with the setting sun.

Stan stopped outside a storefront and used its lights to read the list handed him. It was a new list of names of "outlaw" Soviet officials and military leaders who were gathering military equipment and other material to set up a new government in the mountains between Georgia and Azerbaidzhan. The list was not long, but it was important.

Stan had no idea how Aleks had gotten his information, but he had always been an accurate source.

God! breathed Stan. Is such a thing happening?

The number of nuclear warheads that were missing from Soviet inventory was scary. These people had those "lost" nuclear weapons.

He would later destroy the list. For now he would go home and memorize it. This information would go with him to America.

Stan returned home. His spirits were lighter. He would be leaving all of this worry behind soon. His only worry now was for his children, one of whom was an alcoholic. But those problems would have to be solved at some future time. For now he was happy that he and his lovely Yelena were on their way to a new world and a new life.

3

Stan Styczyski sat in the outer office of John Sikorski at the Central Intelligence Agency headquarters in Langley, Virginia. Stan found Washington, D.C. beautiful, overactive and intimidating. Then he saw the poor sections of the city where the once-beautiful parks and buildings were seedy and badly in need of repair. The ride across the river into Virginia had not changed his feelings. America was even more dynamic and fast-paced than he remembered. The country also seemed more crowded with people and automobiles.

Yelena had been more than willing to leave the failing Soviet Union and start a new life in the United States. But after three nights in America, the farm girl from Ukraine was overwhelmed. The pictures on TV of shootings and other acts of violence in America's own national capitol scared her.

He had returned to America with valuable information about Soviet civilian and military leaders, and although he had not expected to return as a hero, he had expected more attention from the U.S. Government. He had no way of knowing that he would spend the next four weeks isolated from Yelena, being debriefed day after day by a team of specialists. He would later be brought to the office of the head of the C.I.A. and be recognized and decorated for his actions for the benefit of the United States.

John Sikorski entered the outer office from the hall. He had been in a meeting when Stan arrived. John held out his hand to be shaken by Stan. "So, after all these years, we meet again."

"My English, it is not good," explained Stan.

"Then we can speak in Polish or Russian," suggested John.

"Oh, no, that is no necessary. If I am call this country home, then I must learn the language, yes?" asked Stan.

"We need more immigrants to think that way," replied John.

"I have much to tell you," Stan informed him.

"Good. Let's go into my office," invited John. He looked at his secretary. "I think this man deserves a good cup of American coffee."

She smiled an agreement and proceeded to get both men a cup. She brought the cups into the office along with a thermos jug full of hot coffee and sugar and cream on a tray.

"John, there are civilian and military leaders, active duty, who form a new republic," said Stan after the woman left. "They are all from old Soviet Union."

John raised his eyebrows. He had heard rumors, but that was all they had been. Many confused rumors about the remains of the Soviet Union and the new commonwealth of independent republics were flooding over the town and flowing like booze at a political function.

"This is true. They have weapons—many—some atomic.

They get tanks. They get artillery cannons. They have men. They take it all south and now they will get land, their own republic,'' insisted Stan.

John stood up and asked, ''Where?''

''They take it from Azerbaidzhan and Armenia. Maybe they take the Nagorno-Krabakh back again and run all Christians out,'' Stan told him.

A frown knotted John's forehead. ''Are you sure?'' he asked, then he raised his hand. ''Of course you're sure or you wouldn't be telling me this.''

John looked hard at Stan, and then his eyes shifted to the map of the U.S.S.R. on the wall of his office. He said slowly, ''The leaders of Azerbaidzhan are arming for war themselves. Armenia would also object to anyone taking over part of their republic. That new group barging in on them could cause a war between them. With nukes involved, that could mean trouble for the rest of the world. We have people to talk to.''

Stan agreed with him. He had been waiting to tell someone he trusted completely. John Sikorski, a fellow Pole, was that person. He asked hesitantly, not wanting to impose upon John, but he had to ask, ''My children, can they be brought here, to America?''

''I think that will be arranged,'' John informed him.

''How will I live here in this beautiful country, America? I am a sixty-eight-year-old man with little or no American,'' said Stan honestly.

''You, my Polish friend, will stay with the C.I.A. until you retire. You should retire soon. I also. Then you will retire on pension of the U.S. Government. We take care of our own, Stan. Remember that,'' John informed him. He got up to leave, saying, ''Let's go do it.''

John spent five hours with Stan and other experts on the Soviets. By the time he left and went back to his office, he believed what Stan Styczyski was telling them.

He called the head office. He told them what he had learned and then said, "Yes, sir, I'll be right up."

John picked up the notes from his desk and called for his secretary. She entered and he told her, "I'll be upstairs in the Chief's office. I don't want to be bothered by anyone until I give the word. No calls from anyone except Stan Styczyski."

"Yes, sir," she replied, closing the door behind them as John left the office.

John Sokol, personal advisor to the President of the United States, read the report from the Central Intelligence Agency. He had asked for and received a briefing on the matter of former Soviet officials breaking away from the republics and forming their own country. He was doubtful of the information at first, but after a detailed briefing, he believed.

Sokol buzzed the chief of staff and said, "I've got to see the President. The N.S.C. advisor needs to be there."

"He has a tight schedule," the voice over the phone started.

"He'll have a tighter schedule if he doesn't get a tight hold on this thing immediately," growled Sokol. "I'm on my way now."

John Sokol was a businessman who had arrived from Albania with his parents with little more than they had on their backs or carried in hand bags. He had become wealthy by sheer drive and force of personality. No one intimidated John Sokol, especially professional politicians.

The President looked up from the report and said, "These guys are serious, aren't they?"

"They're hacked off about losing their status as leaders of a superpower. Can't blame 'em too much," said John.

"I need a finding, General," the President directed the head of N.S.C. "And alert Fire Storm."

The General nodded, a serious look on his face, and left to notify the commanding general of the Special Operations Command that the Eagle Attack Team may have a mission.

"Damn! The cold war ends and we still have problems," the President grumbled.

"Did you expect less?" asked John.

The President grinned wryly, "Not really, John. Not as long as there are people alive who seek power."

"I've got work to do," explained John as he rose from his seat.

"Since I'm making you head of this thing, you better believe you have work to do," agreed the President. "I want to be kept informed about everything."

As John left the room, he signaled to the President that he would be kept informed. John Sokol knew well the President's interest in foreign affairs. He also knew that the members of the Eagle Attack Team were always ready and waiting for a mission. It seemed the more involved the mission, the happier they were. Well, their government had a very complicated mission for them this time.

4

Vladimir Bokey, head of the old Soviet Union's Interior Ministry's (MVD) "black berets," stood and watched the men walk toward him. The four walked across the snow in their heavy winter boots. Spring would come, but not soon enough for Vladimir. It would be warmer in the south, except in the mountains where they were going.

Three of the four men were of middle years. The third man was younger but wise in the teachings of Marx and Lenin. He was a true believer in Red domination of the world.

"Ah, Vladimir, are you well?" called Pyotr Kolchak, a Don Cossack. The old Cossack had been a staunch Communist when other Cossacks had resisted. He had worked for the G.P.U., which became the K.G.B. in 1953, as an informant on his own people during Stalin's purges. He was trusted by all Soviets who worked with him, for he had no place else to go. His outward appearance of good naturedness belied his nearly criminally insane streak. He was a brutal, expert interrogator who felt no compassion for anyone. And he had many years of experience in brutalizing his fellow man.

Vladimir nodded his head at the men and returned with, "Pyotr, you look well for an old man."

"Ah, I think all of us are beyond our prime," he said, and then pointed toward the younger man. "Except maybe for our young Colonel Georgi Krasnov."

Georgi Krasnov, late of the Red Army, was an expert in artillery and nuclear weapons' delivery systems. He didn't look up or acknowledge that he was being spoken about. He was a serious-minded man who had no time for pleasantries.

Dmitri Lurye and Ivan Ryumin followed. Dmitri had been in the Soviet Ministry of Defense. Ivan had been in the Ministry of Transportation and was the most important of all to Vladimir. Without a good transportation system to move equipment and men south, their plan would have already fallen apart.

The men gave brief greetings. They all had known each other for many years. Each man also know they were playing a very serious and dangerous game. They were in a win-all or lose-all situation.

"Lunin will not come in with us," Vladimir announced. Vladimir Lunin was a former Red Army field marshal.

"The failed coup by his friends still scares the old man," growled Georgi. "He fears being found out, as if he were young enough to worry about what they might do to him."

"Some men like the last few years of their lives quiet and unadventurous." Dmitri Lurye spoke for the first time.

"That is true," replied Pyotr, who had seen many men suffer unspeakable horrors before they died.

"It is no problem," Vladimir assured him. "We have all the leaders we need. And Lunin will not give us away. He fears us more than he fears the new Russian regime."

"Fear is needed to keep law and order among the masses," Georgi said. He was by Red Army standards a man of great technical education and knowledge, but when it came to power, he was as brutal as the Don Cossack he traveled with.

"That is a great truth," agreed Pyotr. He gave a vulgar laugh and said, "If he betrays us and I catch him, I will cut off that useless thing between his legs."

"Enough of this," Vladimir ordered. He was the unofficial leader of the group. "We will be ready to set up our southern headquarters in two days. We have places ready for families for those who wish to take them. I think most will leave their families behind. Colonel, will you explain what you have accomplished?"

"Yes, Comrade. We have barracks for one hundred thousand men within a ten-mile radius. There are facilities for another one hundred and fifty thousand men in so-called primitive facilities. That is enough for two hundred and fifty thousand men," Georgi informed them. "Most of the men I will try to enlist to our cause are veterans of Afghanistan or former advisors to Nicaragua, Cuba, Vietnam, Angola and other places the world over. They're used to primitive facilities. We have sixty thousand men at the camps already. Plus many from Georgia wish to join us. We will get the rest, believe me."

"We can't keep all of this secret much longer," Ivan reminded them. "How have we gone this long?"

"No, we can't. But no one knows that we have nine of the missing nuclear warheads. When they find that out—and we will tell them at the appropriate time—then it will give everyone pause," grinned Vladimir. It wasn't a pleasant grin, but one that was evil. This man would blackmail the world for what he wanted and then destroy it if he was denied or threatened with capture. Saddam Hussein was a pussycat next to this man.

"It is amazing that the West knows nothing of the construction and movement going on in the mountains!" exclaimed Dmitri.

"Ah, the Americans control the spy machines of the West. And they want to believe in peace," spat Georgi in disgust. "What do their politicians call for now that the Union has broken up? Not a strong army they may need for troubled times in the future, for times when strong men of vision try to control this part of the world. They want peace dividends from the end of the Cold War to use at home for their own political advancement. American politicians make political votes with their loud, whimpering call for peace and isolation. The American people want peace and a small military at all costs. That decadent nation will fall when we get through with them."

"That is true. The Americans are a great disappointment. They are not the great world leaders they believe themselves to be. They have the world at their feet and they talk about peace and brotherhood," agreed Vladimir. "They think the world is so at peace with itself that they have even canceled most of their overflights by manned aircraft. They depend upon their satellite cameras to tell them what they want to know about us. Anyone can fool a camera in the sky. Look what Hussein did. He had nuclear plants in operation, and the Americans couldn't find his positions with their 'spy-in-the-sky' technology."

"Once we get our delivery systems in place, then we'll talk to the Americans and the rest of the world about what we want," Georgi informed them.

"Ah, the look on their faces when they find out we have a nuclear capability and a delivery system in place and ready to use. It will even be worse once they learn that we mean what we say. There won't be enough vodka to wash their fears away,'' laughed Pyotr.

"The majority of the public in America like cocaine,'' Georgi reminded him.

"We must decide something of importance now. Will I get any opposition to being the leader?'' asked Vladimir.

Georgi looked at the other three. The colonel spoke for all of them when he said, "None from us, Vladimir. All you need to do to keep us with you is for you to remember who was with you from the start. We four. It was we four. And we four can cancel anything we have a mind to.''

It was an unveiled threat given by brutal men to an equally brutal man. Vladimir understood. He would not have understood if they had followed him blindly.

"I'll remember that, my comrades,'' agreed Vladimir. "Now, we get ready to go south.''

"Long live the Motherland!'' announced Ivan in a strong voice.

"Agreed! Glory to the Motherland!'' shouted Pyotr. He pulled a flask from his coat pocket, took a long drink, then passed it around.

Four of the men were veterans of the Great Patriotic War, as the Soviets called World War II. They remembered such cries as *"Glory to the Motherland!"* and *"Under the banner of Lenin, forward to victory!"* and *"Glory to the Red Army!"*

Georgi had been too young to remember the great war, but he had been well indoctrinated in the past glories of the Soviets and the Red Army. He called out, "Glory to the Red Army!''

The five men used strong Russian Vodka to seal their declaration to intimidate and cow the world.

5

Truck Grundy received a warning order from Brigadier General Dan Olive. The warning order only stated that the team prepare to move out of the Continental United States on an operation. That winter clothing would be required was added. That was enough for Truck and his men.

"What's up, boss?" asked Bad Bear.

"Dan'll have to fill me in, but we've got an operation outside the U.S. and we need cold weather gear," replied Truck.

"I's ready to lock an' load," was Bad Bear's only comment as he left the office.

Truck looked over at Crackers Grahame and told the retired navy lieutenant, "Get Stu in here."

"Gotcha," said Crackers and left.

"Gotta keep these boys on their toes and keep 'em from going rusty. A good fight now and again will do it," mumbled Truck to himself.

Crackers returned with Stewart Barringer, Lieutenant

Colonel, U.S. Army, Retired, the team's operations officer.

"Stu, we're gonna be leaving for Bragg shortly. You and I'll go," said Truck.

"I'll get ready."

Truck looked back at Crackers and asked, "Is Willie coming in from the Philippines soon?"

"He'll be back in a couple of days," answered Crackers.

"Good. Crackers, get the warning order out. Of course, it'll be for our info only. Make sure all the men have their insurance and wills made out," ordered Truck. "I don't reckon we'll be going to play soldier. I have an idea this exercise will be shootin' for real."

Red Dog Bavaros, Colonel, U.S. Air Force, walked into the room. He walked to the coffee pot, poured and downed a cup of hot coffee without taking the cup down. When he finished his first cup of coffee, he looked around at the other three. He could see the expectation in their faces. He asked Truck, "We got something going?"

"Got a warning order from Olive. That's all I know, except that the operation will take us out of the States and we need cold weather gear," Truck told him.

"We got our birds ready and runnin' just in the nick of time," said Red Dog. "I wouldn't a wanted to miss anything."

"We got all of that new equipment installed and checked out just in time," commented Stu.

"I tell ya, boys, these guys in R and D are coming up with some equipment that is *it* in capitol letters," said an appreciative Red Dog. "They got equipment that woulda been so damned heavy it woulda taken a C-130 to haul it all around a few years ago, that is if anybody coulda come up with some of this stuff we've got now. Hell, that Blackhawk of Truck's carries just about everything a 747 used to haul around. That's miniaturization."

"Not only has the size and weight been cut down, can you imagine an instrument reading concentrated atomic stuff while up in the air in an aircraft?" put in Crackers. "That means it has to separate the radioactive emissions put out by the manmade stuff and that made by nature. And it'll pinpoint a warhead as small as a 105mm artillery round."

"Yeah, but it's got to be out of its protective lead case and ready to fire before it'll pick it up," stated Red Dog.

"I still tell ya, boys, that what we've got in instruments is an advancement over any and everything that's been done in the past twenty years," said Crackers.

"I've gotta go along with that," agreed Red Dog.

"We're on our way to Bragg," Truck broke in. "When we get our mission, we'll get back and make up an ops plan."

"I are ready for action," put in Red Dog. "This sittin' around is for the birds an' old ladies."

They hadn't been back from Desert Storm too many months. They had had a little clean-up work to do over there before they returned to their home base.

Truck picked up his briefcase and Stu followed him out the door of the office. They left the hangar that was guarded twenty-four hours a day and went to the Bachelor's Officer Quarters to get ready to leave.

Dan's aide-de-camp filled the thermos coffee pitcher as soon as he saw Truck and Stu walk in. The general's secretary buzzed General Olive that Truck and Stu had arrived.

Dan swung the door open and greeted Truck and Stu, "You got here in a hurry."

"You said haul and we're ready," Truck informed him after a handshake and a Special Forces bear hug.

Dan repeated the greeting with Stu. He turned back into

the office and said, "Come on in. We've got some talking to do."

The aide placed the coffee pitcher down and left the office.

"What we got, Dan?" asked Truck.

"Trouble in the old Soviet Union," said Dan.

"Well, I'm sure glad you let me in on that," Truck said in a sour voice. That was all the world had been hearing about for months.

"No, I mean we've got a problem that could intimidate the entire world," explained Dan. He looked from Truck to Stu. "There's a group of ex-Soviet officials who can't bear losing the power and perks they had under the old regime. There's a group who has access to nuclear warheads and delivery systems. They have a number of both warheads and missiles. How many, I don't know yet. Sullivan is in Washington getting all the info we need."

"A group of nuts have a nuclear capability?" asked Truck. He had been expecting something like this to happen when the Soviet Union fell apart.

"That, plus hundreds of tanks and artillery pieces. They're ready to make war on someone. They're located down south somewhere. I place them in the Caucasus countries," Dan told them.

Truck, an expert in geography, mused a moment and said, "That'd be Georgia, Azerbaidzhan or Armenia. Any of those countries have enough problems already. They damned sure don't need an outlaw Red Army among 'em."

"That's a fact," said Dan.

Stu nodded in agreement, but he let the other two men talk. He poured himself and the other two more coffees.

"You two get set up at the place where you're staying, and I'll let you know as soon as General Sullivan returns," Dan told them.

"We'll be ready," said Truck.

"Stu, I've set you up with a room at the BOQ, if that's what you want," said Dan, then he looked at Truck and said with a smile, "I expect you'll be staying with Dot."

Truck gave a sour face, "Ain't fornication, adultery and things like that against regs in this army anymore?"

"Only if you're caught," grinned Dan. "And who the hell is gonna be dumb enough to check in on Dot Botts and Truck Grundy? Not even your enemies who'd like to fix your wagon are dumb enough for that. Besides, you're both single anyway."

Truck turned and lifted a hand in parting. Stu shook Dan's hand and followed.

"I've also got you a sedan and driver," Dan called to them. There was still laughter in his voice.

Truck called Colonel Dorthy Botts at her office. "I'm in-country and need a place to say," he told her.

"You've always got one, big man," she replied.

"I need a way to get in the house and then I've got some things to do."

"I told you before to take a key."

There was silence on his end of the line.

"Have you got transportation?" she asked.

"Yep."

"Come by the office and I'll give you a key to my quarters," she told him. "And, damnit, keep the thing."

"Yes, ma'am," he replied and hung up the phone.

After stowing his gear at Dot's quarters on main post, Truck went to the United States Army John F. Kennedy Special Warfare Center's library and read as much as he could find on the breakup of the Soviet Union. He knew he would get a classified report on the country he was going to be involved with, but he wanted more about the Soviet Union as a whole as it was falling apart and the new evolving republics. The library at JFKSWC on Smoke Bomb Hill at Fort Bragg, North Carolina, was one of the best in the army, maybe the entire U.S. military.

While he was studying material on current events in the old Soviet Union, Dan's office called to tell him that Sullivan had returned from Washington and they were to meet in the office of the CG, United States Joint Special Operations Command.

General Bryan Sullivan, U.S. Army, CG, USJSOC, had called ahead on a secure line, and everything was set up and ready when he walked into the command's War Room. He was followed by Dan, Truck and Stu.

Maps of the southern Caucasus area with the countries of Azerbaidzhan, Armenia and Georgia were on A-frames about the room. A colonel, a major and a six-stripe sergeant were the only ones in the room.

Sullivan sat down and spoke to the colonel in front of the room who held a long pointer, "Okay, Bill, let's get it on the road."

"From the information you handed me when you returned from Washington just minutes ago, General, I've got this for you," Bill told him. He looked at Truck, Dan and Stu to include them in the briefing. "This is the center of the location where the outlaw Red Army is setting up."

Bill pointed to an area in the mountains between Azerbaidzhan and Armenia. Bill continued, "They are located southeast of Lake Sevan and spread out in an area of several kilometers in size. They have their command split up into five areas, each supported by the other. They are reported to have seventy-five thousand or more men. Tanks, up to two hundred. Artillery, up to two hundred and fifty pieces. Missiles, ten long range and fifteen short range, that we have intel on. We don't know anything about their air support. There are no planes in the immediate area, so they must be located in other areas to be flown in on command. We cannot say that these numbers are accurate.

"We believe that a man named Vladimir Bokey, who was once in the Soviet Ministry of the Interior, is their leader. By the way, all of the positions of these people will be either in the old Soviet Union Government or the Red Army. And we're not sure if these are their real names or their *noms de guerre*. There is also an Ivan Ryumin, once a member of the Ministry of Transportation. A Dmitri Lurye, once a member of the Ministry of Defense. And one person we do know; a Colonel Georgi Krasnov, artillery, Red Army. He is an expert in nuclear devices and delivery systems. With him along, we have a problem, because he knows his business."

"What do Azerbaidzhan and Armenia have to say about these guys moving in on them?" asked Truck.

"They don't like it, but there are too many Reds under arms for them to do anything right now. And we're not even sure if they know the scope of the invasion into their territory. There are also hard-line Communists in the two countries that will be behind the Red Army when the balloon goes up," Bill informed him. He paused, then continued, "This bunch was good on their tactical move into the Caucasus. They kept an entire army hidden from all eyes as they were moving in, and then suddenly they appeared. They go where they want to in the south, so it seems."

"Those people in Azerbaidzhan are Moslems for the most part. They're devout types who kneel toward Mecca to pray five times every day, and they kept their faith and religious traditions even with the Commies in control. They thought they were getting rid of a heathen, godless bunch when the Red Soviets fell, and now these guys move in. I bet that bunch in Baku are fit to be tied,'' said Sullivan.

''Do we have an ally?'' asked Truck.

''We don't know. We're checking it out,'' the general told him.

''We got a report that a group of hard-line Communists, all armed and once part of the Red Army, were moving out of Georgia and heading south. That must be where they were going,'' said Dan.

''Goddamn! Twenty or more nuclear warheads and that many delivery systems!'' spat Sullivan. ''Where were those guys in Russia who were supposed to be controlling those things?''

''Trying to jockey for positions of power,'' said Truck. ''Now it'll be up to someone with a big set of balls to go in and dislodge this crazy bunch.''

''That's where you high-paid guys come in,'' Sullivan told them.

The President wanted the Eagle Attack Team ready to neutralize the situation that had been allowed to develop in the former Soviet Union. When the proper time arrived, the United States would contact the republics involved for clearance and offer any help needed. If permission could not be gotten, they would go on their mission the way they had gone on all others in the past. They would go covert, with no markings on their equipment, and they would do what had to be done, then return to their secured area at Fort Hood to await their next call from the President of the United States.

All information that was now available would be kept under wraps. They didn't want to alert the outlaw Red Army that they had been found out. Let them stay dumb and happy with the thought that the United States didn't know or care what was going on in the rest of the world.

It was 1900 hours by the time General Sullivan called it

a day. They would continue to work on the problem tomorrow. All facilities would be available to the team as per usual.

The sun had set by the time Truck left HQ and went to join Dot at the Officer's Club for supper.

6

Truck let Stu have the use of the sedan for the night. Dot had her own car if they needed one, and she lived within walking distance of the main Officer's Club.

There were a number of officers in the club who Truck knew from the past. Most of them were now field grade officers and near retirement. Time passed and men got older. Only the army, with its many traditions, stayed the same. Those traditions were not spoken or written about as much as they were in the British or other foreign armies. But they were there. The tradition of brotherhood of the officer's corps. The tradition of the valued assets of wives and children to the army, to the home, to the man and his career were still there. Army traditions had taken a beating since World War II with the large influx of citizen soldiers. But now that the army was being reduced in size, those traditions would return and be embraced by both the officers and the enlisted men. Tradition was part of being a professional soldier. Truck thought sometimes it was the best part.

A colonel walked over to their table. He grinned, "Well, well, ole Truck Grundy is still alive and kicking."

"Howdy, Vic," Truck said and stood up to shake Victor Terrel's hand. "Glad to see you got your eagle."

"Hi, Dot," Vic said. He turned back to Truck and said, "I wouldn't have gotten this far if I hadn't had officers like you to teach me the ropes when I got out of West Point. You know, Dot, me and this old boy go way back. We were in Germany together, I was a second lieutenant, and we've crossed paths many times since. Some of those times have been in some strange places."

"Yep, they have been. You're about ready to retire, aren't you?" asked Truck.

"Next week. I was ready to retire before Desert Storm, but there was no way I was going to leave the army with that thing in the mill," said Vic. "I've just finished writing up after-action reports of the war and helped set up some training exercises for what we learned. But I'll hang it up and let the younger generation take over."

"And I don't remember ever being as young as some of these guys," laughed Truck.

"Me neither. But we *are* looking at them through different eyes now," Vic reminded him.

"Yeah, much older eyes."

"I'd sure hate to be just starting out in the army business right now. I'd get bored as hell knowing I might spend thirty years and not fight a war the entire time," Vic said.

"I've heard that said a lot lately," Truck told him.

"Yeah, so have I." Vic raised a hand and said, "Got to get back home. I was here having supper with a couple of young lieutenants I have in my section. I remember you used to do that with us young guys."

"See ya around," Truck said.

Dot planted a parting kiss on his cheek and Vic left.

"The old ones are fading away," Truck said in clipped words.

"Time will do that, I suppose. I haven't gotten there yet," Dot smiled.

"Live long enough and it'll happen to you also," he assured her.

They finished their meal and took the short walk to Dot's quarters. The house was a two-story family-sized unit, but since she was a full colonel, she qualified for such a large house.

Dot went to the bar and poured both of them a glass of cognac. She joined him on the sofa.

"Thanks, lady," replied Truck, accepting the glass.

She raised her glass in a toast. "To the United States of America and its army."

"I'll drink to that," said Truck.

After the toast, Dot asked, "Are you here on business?"

"I'm always on business," Truck informed her.

"I mean team business. Are you going somewhere on an operation?"

"I'm here because Dan Olive called me."

"That doesn't answer my question," she told him.

Truck took a drink from his glass. She had been involved in three operations because her expertise was needed. She didn't have anything extra to offer on this mission and he would not discuss it with her.

His silence perturbed her and she asked, "You're not going to tell me, are you?"

He ignored her. She already knew the answer.

She sat a moment. She had known Truck Grundy long enough to understand that when he decided to do something or not to do something, there was no moving him. Neither sex nor intimidation would move this man. Knowing she wouldn't get anything out of him, she changed the subject to current affairs, hoping she might hit upon something.

"Now that the Soviet Union no longer exists, I suppose Congress will cut the military back to nothing," she said.

"Be about like those politicians. They cut us back after World War II and we went into Korea without enough men or the proper equipment. They had to fly special equipment over to us. But take a look at history. It never fails. Once the threat is over, the country regresses back into itself. The soldier becomes less important and equipment he needs even more so. When trouble starts again, their sons have to suffer because some politician made political hay out of the situation," growled Truck. "And I'm getting tired as hell of hearing about damned peace dividends."

"Do you think the new republics will have difficulty with each other now that there is no central government?"

"Might," he answered.

Truck had thought for a long time there was going to be trouble. The new leaders of the new republics were ex-Communists. They were used to strong central control of everything their people did. Truck figured most of them would preach democratic rule, but in reality they would be nothing but dictators or their countries would be ruled by some other type of autocracy.

He had also believed that some of those in power in the Soviet Union would try to keep things as they were. The only way to gain control of a country to their way of thinking would be by military force. They were not pro-grammed to think any other way.

"They could use more of our military for drug interdiction," she said.

"Might as well," said Truck in agreement with the idea. "It would give the military a training ground for some of their new equipment and keep other units operating as an organization.''

"You don't think they'll use your people on such an operation, do you?''

"I don't have the foggiest,'' he told her.

They were silent a moment.

"I enjoyed my visit to San Antonio with your family,'' said Dot, changing the subject. "And, yes, I did like your sister.''

"Ruth's a tough ole gal,'' Truck told her.

"She said that's what you thought about me,'' she laughed. "I take that as a compliment, coming from you.

"But I do wish Linn could have been there.''

"Yep. Glad she made it back from the desert,'' agreed Truck. His daughter, Linn, was in the army reserves as a helicopter pilot. She had been called up for the war and had flown missions in Iraq. When reports came out about some female pilot being shot down or crashing, a catch in his throat would cut off air to his lungs for a few moments. But she had come back in good health. Before she left he had told her she would, stating that the old Grundy luck would hold for her as well as it had for him and his brothers when they had been in wars.

"Truck, I'm still thinking about asking for a transfer to Headquarters at Fort Hood. That'll put us closer to each other. I'm sure I can get a release from here,'' she told him.

"I'd think about it more if I were you,'' he told her. "You're on your way to making a star if you stay here. This is the place where all the action is. And every CO I've talked to likes your work and has only praise for you.''

"I can do just as well at Hood as I can here.''

"Yeah, you can. But there's a difference. Doing well in this job you're in now will get you that star," he insisted. "I know, you'd give up that star to come to Hood. But I would rather see you make general before you retire. You deserve it."

"I miss being with you." she complained. She moved over closer to him.

She smelled good to Truck. She felt even better. He didn't know how much longer this relationship was going to last before he gave up and married this lady. He could do worse. In fact, he had done worse before. He knew that his job taking him away from her on a moment's notice and maybe for long periods of time would not come between them. She was an old trooper herself and understood the meaning of the word duty. Duty, Honor, County! That said it all.

She blew in his ear.

"Blood heating up, huh?" he asked.

"I've been hot since the first time I saw you, big man."

"And you've acted like it."

"Is there a complaint?" she asked. She pressed a breast up against his arm. She knew he liked the feel of her.

"Nope," he said. He downed the drink and stood up. "Are you going to walk up those stairs, or am I going to carry you?"

She smiled, placed her glass on the coffee table and stood up. "You are such a romantic. Off with your clothes and into bed without a pause. A woman likes to be made love to and not jump straight into bed."

He started for the stairs. He looked back over his shoulder and said, "Maybe for some, but not all. You usually beat me to bed."

She continued to smile and told him, "I'll be up in a

minute. I want to put these glasses away and check on my schedule for tomorrow.''

"I'll be busy tomorrow. I'll let you know if we can have lunch or not,'' he said, continuing up the stairs. He wanted her more than he let on. He was sure that she knew that.

7

Truck, Dan and Stu met in General Sullivan's office. Colonel Rufus Holguin, U.S. Army, and Truck's one-on-one, was also present. The general was fuming over the message he had received from Washington. The content of the message informed him to have the Eagle Attack Team stand down until further notice.

"Goddamn!" growled Sullivan. "Just like this problem is going to go away. We need to cut those Reds off before they get set up and ready to start a war. I got Sokol on the line and asked him what the hell was going on. From the gist of our conversation, the White House don't want to upset Russia and the other republics by even offering to take care of the problem for them. Now ain't that one hell of a note?"

"That sounds like it came straight out of the State Department," said Truck.

Dan looked at Truck and then suggested, "Okay, so we stand down. But we also go on and plan this thing as if it were a go. That way we'll be ready if anything does pop."

"Agreed," said Truck with a nod of his head.

Sullivan downed the last of his coffee and told them, "Okay, keep planning as if it's a go. We're Boy Scouts and we are always prepared. We all know that we'd better be prepared. If Washington gets a call for help, they won't care if we were told to stand down or not. They'll only want us to be ready when they call."

The general got up and walked to his desk. He picked up an order and handed it to Truck. "This makes it official."

Truck read it and passed it on to Stu. After reading it, he passed it to Holly. The order would be placed in the classified file of the Eagle Attack Team. That file was marked TOP SECRET, EYES ONLY.

"You boys know what to do. That's what we're paying you all that money for. We use your high-powered expertise when we can't do it out in the open," the general reminded them. He looked at Truck and said, "Truck, you old one-eyed reprobate, if this thing does turn sour, which I know it will, and goes down, I expect you'll be able to handle it as you always have."

"I'll give it my best shot, sir," said Truck as he stood up.

"Then go do it," was Sullivan's order.

The four men left the office.

"Goddamned politicians," growled Sullivan to the empty room. "I thought the President was going to stand tough on this Soviet business."

He was sure that the President and his men were stopped because of lack of communication with the new republics. This president wasn't going to charge anywhere unless he had all concerned behind him. The Gulf War had shown everyone that. But there were times when a leader went on his own, against the grain and common wisdom. "Give 'em Hell" Truman had gone against advice to the contrary during the Korean War. He committed American troops and then asked the U.N. to give its blessing. It seemed the old boy didn't give a damn whether the U.S. Congress gave their blessings are not. If Truman had waited like the President was doing now, all of Korea would be under Communist control right now.

Something would pry the White House loose. He just hoped it wouldn't be too late.

Truck, Stu and Holguin spent the rest of the day coordinating possible avenues they would need to get to the Caucasus region. Turkey was a possibility. They had used a base in Turkey during the Gulf War. As always, the Turks had been willing to work with the United States on any adventure that called for armed conflict. Their willingness to stand with the United States was a hell of a lot more than you could say for some so-called allies.

Holguin and Stu made up a possible cost-analysis report, and when they were finished, they doubled it. They had no idea what they might run into. Then Holguin requested a voucher for the money so that it could be placed in a bank at a later date for withdrawal by the team as it was needed.

"I have an idea things will break sooner than later," Truck told Stu and Holguin.

"I agree," said Stu.

Holguin nodded in agreement.

The three understood what Sullivan and Dan were concerned about. If this outlaw armed force was allowed to set up its nuclear capability and get its firing plans in order, it would have all of Europe and most of the world under threat of nuclear devastation if it didn't get what it wanted. If that was allowed to happen, then it would be too late to react.

Truck called Dan about transportation back to Hood. Dan said it was set up. All they had to do now was get as much information on the probable area of operations. They would finish their ops plan once they got back to Hood.

Truck called Dot late that afternoon.

"Do you already have a flight schedule with the airlines this time of day?" she asked.

"No. General Sullivan has made his plane available."

"And you're leaving this afternoon?"

"Yep."

"Do we have time to go by the house?" she asked.

"I've already got my gear from your quarters. Me and Stu are going by the SF Memorial and then out to the airfield," he told her.

"I'm coming out to see you off," she told him, then paused. "Truck, can I go?"

"I don't think so on this one," he told her. There was no give in his voice. "See ya at the field."

"Okay," she said and hung up. There was an empty spot in her stomach. She knew that something was up, but she knew that she wouldn't be a part of this operation. For some reason it scared her, for she had no idea where he might be going. The world was supposed to be at peace. Wasn't that what the President and Congress were telling the people?

She told her secretary that she was leaving and wouldn't be back until tomorrow. She knew that once she saw Truck off, she wouldn't be worth two cents for the rest of the day.

The American lieutenant colonel took the envelope out of his briefcase and handed it to the CIA representative at the Pentagon. "I was given this by the CIA station chief in Moscow. Since I was on my way out, he asked me to hand it to you. He said it was important and should be handled ASAP."

Bob Watson looked at the envelope addressed to John

Sikorski. He told the army man, "I'll get it over to him right away."

Bob called for a driver and personally carried the letter to Langley.

John Sikorski opened the envelope. There was a letter inside the larger envelope addressed to him. There was a smaller envelope addressed to Stan Styczyski. John called for Stan Styczyski to be brought to his office.

John looked up as Stan entered the office. He greeted him with an, "Ah, glad to see you. Have you been well?"

"I could stand more sleep and to see my wife," complained a tired Stan Styczyski.

"I'll see to that," John told him. He then handed the envelope to Stan. "I just received this from Moscow. I'm sure our Station Chief in Moscow has read it."

Stan nodded his head and opened the envelope. He quickly read the message from Aleksandr, his contact in Moscow. He looked quickly at John and said, "This is urgent business. Poland and Hungary needs to know this information."

"What is it?"

"The Red Army is going to threaten Poland and Hungary with nuclear weapons if they don't help them convince Russia, Ukraine and the rest of Europe that the Red Army in the Caucasus Mountains is the military power of the region," Stan told him.

"What? This is plain blackmail!" cried John.

"This is what I've been trying to tell your people. This is what this is all about," Stan said tiredly.

"When will this happen?" asked John.

"Not soon. Maybe a few weeks, but who knows? They will have to have time to set up their forces and get their delivery systems into place," Stan informed him.

"Can this man who contacted you be counted upon?" asked John. "Where'd he get the information?"

"I have worked with him for over twenty-five years. He has always given me good information. Knowing the people involved in the Red Army, I would believe this information to be correct in any case."

"How does he get all this information?" John wondered.

"This man is an expert in electronics and in bugging offices and homes. I'm sure he has his ways, even now in this so-called democratic Russia," Stan told him. Aleks had given him lessons on countering eavesdropping devices and had found bugs planted in his own apartment. It had angered him when one was found in his bedroom. A man and woman couldn't grunt and groan in their love-making without some counterintelligence man or woman listening to them. God, what a country to live in! But now that was all behind him. He was now in a different world. He was ready to help this newfound world in any way he could.

"It seems you're not sure that the Russian government will stay democratic or not," said John. He offered Stan a cup of coffee.

Stan gratefully accepted the cup of coffee. He took a sip and then told John, "I am never sure of anything when a Russian is involved. Especially if that Russian is a former follower of the great Satan, Lenin. And you must remember, every leader in the republics was at one time a hardened Communist. All of them were in the Red Party and all of them have helped send their friends off to the Gulag. No, I do not trust a one of them."

John nodded his head in agreement. He picked up the phone and dialed. When he got his party on the other end of the line, he said, "Let Stan Stycyski have a few days with his wife."

He listened a moment and then said, ''I don't give a damn what your boss wants. Give him time off or I'll get it for him.'' He placed the phone back on its cradle.

''Thank you,'' Stan said quietly.

''I have many things to do,'' said John. ''All I ask of you is for you to be reachable if I need you.''

Stan nodded his head that he understood. He left the office knowing that he would be able to sleep with his beloved Yelena tonight.

When Stan left the office, John picked up the phone for another call. He said, ''Sokol, I need to see the President—soonest. The Director and I will be right over.''

''I'll see if I can get you in,'' said John Sokol.

''Don't see, set it up,'' replied John.

''It's that hot, huh?''

''Have you ever known me to lie or exaggerate?''

Sokol said it would be done. He wondered what the CIA had for them now. Things were confusing enough in the world without that bunch finding things under the bed.

8

Alex Mikolajczyk, the Polish Ambassador to the United States, and Bela Metzger, Hungarian Ambassador to the United States, met with the American Secretary of State. They had just been informed by their governments that an outlaw Red Army group was going to threaten both countries with annihilation if they did not support the planned military coup.

"The military coup against who?" Bela asked.

"We are not having trouble with any of the old Soviet republics," Alex informed the Secretary of State. "Now this so-called Red Army comes forth. We don't know who or what it is."

"I don't know who these people are or who they represent either, but I will find out," the American informed the two ambassadors.

"I wish to see your President, immediately," requested Alex.

"And I also," put in Bela.

"I'll do my best to find out what is going on and get back to you," the Secretary told them.

"No, Mister Secretary, we will find out what is going on and get with your President," Alex Mikolajczyk shot back. "We are talking about my country. I will not wait on anyone."

"Nor I," put in Bela Metzger.

"I'll contact the White House immediately," the Secretary said, and buzzed his secretary. "Get James Rogers in here, quickly."

He turned to the two excited ambassadors and told them, "Mister Rogers will get things moving, quickly."

The two ambassadors thanked him and left to prepare for their meeting with the President of the United States.

Information about the outlaw Red Army and its plan to blackmail the rest of the world with the threat of nuclear war was kept within a small circle. This small circle of men and women in the governments of the United States, Poland and Hungary was more excited than it had ever been in the past. Some members were near hysteria. The electricity was high and struck like bolts of lightning with each bit of new information about the enemy the world faced. Russia would be contacted later.

The National Security Council met and made plans to counter the threat. The NSC didn't have the means within itself to counter anything or anyone, but its members had to do something to make their positions seem as important as they thought they were.

A few planners and high staff from the Department of Defense were called and asked to give their assessments of the situation. The Secretary of Defense in turn alerted the special operations groups that would be the first to counter this new threat.

The U.S. Government was in a tizzy.

* * *

The President called for General Sullivan and John Sokol to meet with him, the Secretary of State and the NSC advisor. They discussed the situation before them with great concern in their voices.

The President looked at his men a moment and said, "I think we need a consensus with the new republics of the old Soviet empire on what action we should take. We should also decide who should be involved militarily as well as diplomatically."

"Yes, sir," agreed State.

"We can set that up," informed the NSC.

"I think we should go balls-to-the-walls and go straight for the Red Army," said John Sokol without hesitation.

All eyes turned to General Bryan Sullivan. He looked impressive with the four stars of his rank on his shoulders and the rows of colorful ribbons on his chest. The Combat Infantry Badge showed that he had been in combat as a junior infantry officer. His silver jump wings showed he was a qualified paratrooper.

"I don't think we need to get that involved diplomatically with the other states either, Mister President," Sullivan said slowly.

State's eyebrows shot up. NSC looked stoic, waiting for the general to make his point. John waited, knowing that he was going to agree with the general before the man even spoke.

"Please tell me why we should pass all the diplomatic channels," the President said.

"Simple, sir. All we need to do to neutralize this bunch is knock out their nuclear capability," the general informed him.

"But they'll still have a large number of men, tanks, artillery and maybe aircraft," insisted the President.

"They will be neutralized by their location and by the surrounding military forces of Azerbaidzhan and Armenia. Those two countries probably don't like this group any more than the rest of the world," Sullivan told them.

"I like it," John spoke up.

"What we have to worry about is Iran getting into the act if this is not handled quickly," State told the President.

"How about Turkey?" asked the President.

The men looked at each other. Finally Sullivan said, "Turkey will stand down as long as we are doing something. I trusted her during the Gulf War, which proved to be true, and I trust her now to do what is in the best interest for both herself and us. But if we piddle-diddle about, Mister President, they're going to look out after their own interests. Those two countries we're talking about, Azerbaidzhan and Armenia, are just north of their border. They've had to watch their two neighbors, Iraq and Iran, fight it out over the years, which would make most anyone nervous. Now they are also having trouble with the Kurds within their borders. I think they've been damned patient with the rest of the world."

The President looked to the other three. None of them offered any disclaimers to what the general had told them.

"Why would the Red Army want to start with Poland and Hungary?" asked the President.

"General Sullivan and I were talking about that," John told him. "We pretty well decided that those two countries are a threat to them because Poland and Hungary's democratic forms of government are working. Plus, both of them are having a better economic reform than the rest of the old Communist Bloc. As long as the people are happy, have plenty of food and a little extra to enjoy themselves in everyday life, they will not want to return to Communist rule. The two ambassadors from those countries also feel that is true.''

"Damn!" spat the President in disgust. He sat a moment and then said, ''Would all of you leave me with John and General Sullivan a moment?''

The other three men got up and walked out of the office. They hovered near the door, knowing that they would be recalled after the President was finished.

The President looked at the two men and said, ''Both of you worked together before on an operation using our special team. Let's do it again. John, go to both Poland and Hungary and see if they are ready and willing to give assistance with ground troops.''

"He shouldn't go to any of the old Soviet republics, Mister President,'' Sullivan put in quickly.

"I agree with him. They're heavily infiltrated with KGB and GPU people. We'll go to the Russians last,'' said John. He paused and then said, ''We didn't let you down the last time. We won't this time.''

"Do it,'' was the President's order.

Sullivan saluted and left before the President could change his mind.

John smiled and followed the general. He told the three men in the hall, ''The President wants you. And I see the Secretary of Defense has arrived.'' He waved at the Secretary of Defense and kept following the general.

"We gotta get out of this damned place before someone changes the President's mind,'' growled Sullivan.

"Yes, diplomats have a way of looking at the real world differently from the rest of us,'' smiled John.

The two men walked down to John's office where he called for his chauffeur, and they left the White House grounds. Neither of the men wanted to be available should a countermand of their directions be issued.

Sullivan assured John that the Eagle Attack Team was ready for any mission it might be called upon to perform.

Truck held the UH-60 Blackhawk helicopter steady and watched the six Apaches firing on the fixed targets.

"Get that sonofabitch outta the way, Riggs!" yelled Captain Tomas Hernandez over the air.

"Boy, I'm gonna give you something hard to suck on!" Captain Tyron Riggs called back.

"Hey, man, is it gonna be the black handle of a wrench?" laughed Warrant Officer Arturo Velasco over the air.

"As our fearless leader would say, 'Fuck you and the horse ya rode in on,' my man," called Riggs.

"My, my! You black folks an' Mexican people sho use vile language aroun' heah," Warrant Officer Amos Pylant came out with in his best Southern accent.

"Where in the hell did that guy with the accent come from?" Crackers wanted to know.

A disgusted, "Aw, shit!" came from Red Dog.

Truck didn't worry about the team being heard over the air. They had been given special equipment and their own radio frequencies. The communications equipment was very small in size and had a higher frequency range than most had thought possible to use. They would not be heard by ASA or any other monitoring agency. They sure wouldn't be heard by any outside force when they were in operation.

But enough was enough. Truck ordered, "Okay! Can it."

"Sure thing, boss," was keyed in from six radios.

The new equipment had worked well with only minor adjustments. He was thankful to have WO Fullove working on the team's computers and other electronics.

"Eagle Six! Eagle Six! This is base. We just received a message you will want to see ASAP! Do you copy? Over!"

''This is Eagle Six. I copy and I am coming in. Out!''
Truck banked the Blackhawk and called over the radio to
the team, ''This might be the one, boys, so bring 'em on
home.''

The men rogered his transmission and fell into formation.

9

The hangar had become a den of activity since the message was received from Fort Bragg sixteen hours before. All rolling stock was checked and rechecked. The team had six AH-64 Apache attack helicopters; one UH-60 Blackhawk helicopter; one OV-2 observation, twin-engine, push-and-pull aircraft; three maintenance trucks; three reloading, forward area, all-weather vehicles for rearming and refueling the six Apaches; and one two and a half ton supply truck. There were trailers for the trucks. All equipment and supplies were placed on loading pads and secured for placement on aircraft for transport. Each aircraft and vehicle was painted black.

The men worked as a well-oiled machine to get everything ready. Word-play and cat-calls were heard above the noise, but the work never slowed.

While men took care of their assigned equipment, the command section took care of operation and coordination plans.

Colonel Rufus Holquin, Truck's one-on-one, and Matt Helms, a CIA operative stationed at Fort Bragg who worked with the team, had flown in to meet with Truck and his men.

Command Sergeant Major Willie Falloure, U.S. Army, Retired, had arrived, back from his leave in the Philippines. The presence of the tall, black man was felt by the command section. He was the team's intelligence, medical expert and ground man. He had done it all for many years in the Special Forces on many operations.

Truck looked over his men present in the team's "war room," which also served as the main office inside the secured hangar. Stu and Bad Bear were also present. No matter who was the ranking man in the team, Truck always relied upon Bad Bear as his second-in-command. Anyone who didn't like the idea of a retired warrant officer being second-in-command had to get another job, for he was not welcome in Truck's command.

"Bragg is sending down an SF battalion to work with us," Truck informed the men. "They are experts in the Commie Bloc. A number of them can speak Polish and Hungarian. They will work with any ground units our allies send.

"At present, we can figure on going first to Poland. It seems that Poland is pissed off as hell about her former allies, the Soviets, and this bunch who calls themselves the Red Army of the People. She and Hungary are ready to do anything to help us. So we have free air and land travel anywhere within the borders."

"I sure like Polish gals," smiled Willie.

"You like all and any gals and we know it," said Truck, laughing along with the other men. "Stu and Willie will make up the ops plan after we get through talking with Holly and Matt. If anyone has any input during our planning, come forward and do it."

"I've got a read on CIA agents we can use in Poland, Hungary and even Russia," Matt, the CIA operative, told them. "I'll give you their code names and locations."

"The boys at Langley aim to help, huh?" asked Truck.

"They're as worried as the rest of us," said Matt. "They know they have to give up something if they want to stop this bunch without involving the entire world."

"Smart boys," grumbled Stu.

"Okay. Stu, you've got what you need for a start, so you guys get it done," Truck told the men who would be working on the operations plan. "I'm going out and check on the troops."

"Gotcha, boss," said Stu, picking up paper and maps.

Truck left the men deep in planning. He stepped out into the huge hangar filled with working men and equipment.

"Hey, boss, would ya look at them guys work," laughed WO Wally Burnham, U.S. army, and Apache co-pilot/gunner. His face was smudged with oil and dirt and his rolled up flightsuit sleeves were dirty. He was working as hard as his fellow Apache crews.

The other men continued their work with laughter and called nasty names to each other.

Truck watched Crackers take down his basketball hoop and store it in his Apache. He never went anywhere without his basketball and hoop. As soon as the team landed at a new location, out came the ball, up went the hoop and a game began.

The sergeant in charge of the MP guard for the team's hangar approached Truck. He saluted and said, "Sir, there are two SF officers at the door to see you."

"Okay, Sergeant. I'll come with you," said Truck.

Neither the exterior guard or interior guard would allow anyone to get close to the hangar, let alone peek inside for a quick look. Not only was the team itself classified, nearly every piece of equipment the team used also held the highest security designation.

Truck opened the personnel door and stepped out. Lieutenant Colonel Ralph Dogger and Major David Reidenbach were standing there. They gave the proper code names and Truck shook their hands. He led both of the men into the war room. Truck introduced the two men to all concerned.

"We'll go into Poland and there we'll get ground troops for the operation," Truck told them.

"We've been told of our mission," Colonel Dogger told Truck. His voice was full of self-importance and "we do our part, so go to hell."

Truck paused.

Bad Bear looked from Dogger to Truck. This man was in a hurry to get his ass kicked out of the room. He smiled. He liked physical confrontation as much as drinking beer.

"This man, Stu, and this man, Willie, will go with you," Truck informed Dogger. "They have the communications equipment and codes needed to work with our team."

Dogger looked at the men and turned back to Truck. He stood stiffly and said with no give in his voice, "We work alone and without outsiders. We did our job in the Gulf War without help, we'll do so in this operation also."

"We have a different operating procedure in this team, Colonel. We have code names and frequencies that are highly classified and on a need-to-know basis," Truck told him. He immediately saw the kind of person he was dealing with and his hackles began to rise. This man was a tough, elite trooper who felt that if someone hadn't been where he had been, then it wasn't worth talking about.

"If you know anything about Special Forces, you know that my men are cleared for anything you or anyone else is cleared for in this army," Dogger informed him. His arrogance was threatening to undermine his good will.

Truck was not the arguing kind. Every man did as he thought best, then he lived with the consequences. He picked up the phone and dialed. When Dan Olive came on the other end, Truck told him, "Dan, get this goddamned colonel and major back to Bragg before I ship them back in a box."

"Hold on, Truck. You have a problem?" asked Dan.

"I ain't got problem one, Dan." There was no give in his voice. "But this bastard is stuffed with more than ten pounds of shit in a five pound bag."

"Hand him the phone," Dan told Truck.

"Here, Colonel, your boss," said Truck, handing Dogger the telephone.

"Yes, General," said Dogger.

"I don't know what you did to piss off Truck Grundy, but evidently you made quite an impression," said Dan. "You and Mark get on back to Bragg."

"But, General, we came down here on a military mission, not to babysit a damned group of prima donnas," Dogger said into the mouthpiece.

"What in the hell happened to you, Dogger? One little war and you're the tactical genius of the U.S. Army? The only one who's ever gone to war and done a good job? Goddamn! Boy, you'd better get your act straightened out!" Dan shouted over the phone. "When that old bastard said he'd send you two home in a box, he meant what he said. He went through more shit on one of his tours in the old days than you'll go through during your entire life! Now, salute your betters, keep your goddamned mouth shut, and get on that plane for Bragg. Understood?"

"Yes, General," replied Dogger.

Dan slammed down the telephone before Dogger finished.

Dogger put the phone back on its cradle and looked at Mark. He said, "Let's go."

Without looking back, Dogger walked out of the office and into the hangar.

Mark held out his hand, pulled it back and then made an about face and followed his battalion commander.

The other men looked at Truck. They had not heard the other end of the conversation, but hearing this end was enough to understand what had happened.

The telephone in Truck's office rang. It was the one with the voice scrambler. General Dan Olive usually called on that secure line.

Truck picked up the phone and said, "Yeah?"

"Truck, that guy must have pissed you off," Dan said on the other end.

"Yep."

"What do you want?"

"The boys we used from the Tenth on that operation in Bavaria. If we can't have them, I'll take the boys down in Turkey we used in the gulf," Truck told him.

"Ya got 'em," Dan informed him. "What else, Lord Truck?"

"You're doing a good job," Truck said. There was humor in his voice.

"You're good. The best I've seen. But, Truck Grundy, you are also the biggest pain in the ass I've ever had to deal with. Even when I was a second lieutenant in your command. Damn! We all wanted a piece of old Captain Truck Grundy's ass," Dan told him. "But we also knew that if we lived up to your standards, we'd have it made if we ever got into a shooting war."

"Glad ya made general, Dan," said Truck and hung up the phone.

* * *

An order came down that the SF battalion located in Europe was to provide advisors for the upcoming operation. Men would also come from those SF men located in Turkey. The battalion was to meet American forces in a place to be designated at a later time. The battalion commander of European southern Command and a representative would fly in for a conference with Truck.

Truck read the order sent to him and smiled. No one, certainly not some lieutenant colonel who hadn't seen much action was going to tell him what he would and would not do. Truck said aloud, ''I've paid my dues, buddy. Plus, I'm an old warrior and an elder.''

The men worked to get their equipment ready to load on the two C-5A and C-130 planes the U.S. Air Force Air Commandos always provided them.

10

Colonel Georgi Krasnov stood in front of his headquarters located in a mountain pass. The headquarters was on the east side of the Lesser Caucasus Mountains that ran northwest and southeast through Azerbaidzhan. A short distance to the west, within sight when he climbed to the top of the pass, was the Armenian border. To the east, far below him, was the interior of Azerbaidzhan. They were located about fifty miles south of Kirovabad, the second largest city in Azerbaidzhan, and north of the Terter River. Once out of the mountains, the land in this part of Azerbaidzhan to the east and all the way Caspian Sea, was a flat, fertile plain where large fruit orchards, sheep ranches, grain fields and grapes flourished.

Azerbaidzhan had been called Albania in ancient times. It was also known by the Arabs as Arran. Now it was a nation in turmoil, like so many of the former Soviet republics.

The house used for the headquarters was small, but there were a number of large storage buildings and troop barracks in the immediate area. Guard posts were in place and manned around the headquarters as well as around the main encampment.

The wind coming from the north was cold now, but in a few weeks it would be warm. In the steppes the temperature would rise above one hundred degrees during the day. It would get hot in the mountains during the day, but the temperature would drop quickly as the sun went down.

Georgi stood and watched the troops from Georgia pass by in columns. They were a ragtag bunch of men who had fought against the democratic forces of Georgia. They had little more than a loaf of *lavish*, a soft Georgian bread, in their packs and a few rounds of ammunition. The few vehicles they had were dirty and in bad repair. In appearance, they were a disheartening sight. But if nothing else, they were fellow Communists and would fight to regain control and end this democratic nonsense.

These men from Georgia called their country Sakartvelo. Most of the men in uniform were native to Georgia and had been members of the Red Army stationed in Georgia. Most were also Red Party loyalists. A few of the uniformed men were Russian, Ukrainians and from other republics that had made up the Soviet Union.

A dirty, worn staff car pulled up and stopped in front of Georgi. A man in a Red Army uniform got out of the back of the car and walked up to him. He was a native of Georgia. Georgi greeted him, "Ah, General Zviad Belenko. Welcome to our new command post. I hope we have a place that will meet your approval."

"All I need is a place to rest my weary bones and fill my belly," exclaimed Zviad. "This traveling undercover at night is hard on old men."

Georgi smiled, but there was no humor in his eyes.

A second man got out of the back of the car. He was

bleary eyed, overweight and needed a shave. He stood up and stretched with both arms thrown out. He joined the other two men.

"You have met Dzhaba Groman, our Political Officer," said Zviad.

"Yes, we have met," returned Georgi and held out his hand in greeting.

"What a trip," said an exasperated Dzhaba. The political officer was used to his comforts, his food and his women. He was known to take peasant women from husbands and fathers without a thought of right or wrong. All he knew was that his needs had to be fulfilled at whatever cost to the people.

"I have no girls for you," was Georgi's greeting.

"Ah, such a shame. But I think that can be taken care of," said Dzhaba, looking around at the bleak landscape of mountaintops and valleys in the far distance. "There must be peasant girls even in this god forsaken country. I will not take a female goat."

"There are many Moslem girls in the valleys with the sheep. Of course, you know how these Moslems handle men who take their daughter's maidenheads or violate the sanctity of a married woman," laughed Zviad.

"I have a way of handling such men, and that's with a knife," growled Dzhaba. "When I get through with them, they will not need a woman."

Georgi was tired of such talk. He asked, "How many men do you bring with you?"

"Fourteen thousand. There are two thousand with me on this trip," Zviad told him.

"Will the others get here soon?" asked Georgi.

"Don't worry. They will all be here," Zviad assured him.

"Georgi, our new military leader, you have not changed since I first saw you many years ago," laughed Dzhaba.

"You were a serious-minded man as a junior officer. Rank and responsibility has not dampened the fire in your belly or made you less serious."

"Only with the return of power to our Party and the unification of all of our Motherland will there be rest in my soul," was Georgi's only comment.

Dzhaba shrugged his shoulders. He had met many young ideological men in the past. He was a realist. A Communist, but a realist who wanted only power, not an ideology.

The three men went into the small house Georgi used as his headquarters and as his own personal quarters. He poured all three a glass of vodka and raised his glass in a toast. "To Lenin and the glory of the Motherland!"

The other two men returned the toast and downed their drinks.

"Is this the best you could find for our headquarters?" Dzhaba nearly shouted.

"My dear, Dzhaba, we are now field soldiers, men going to war. We can't chose our fighting place or where we should set up our command post," Zviad told him. There was a hint of contempt in the general's voice.

Dzhaba shrugged his heavy shoulders and poured himself another drink.

"You will have better quarters. It is not far from here, just around the bend in the small hill to the south of headquarters," promised Georgi. "A woman must be of your own doing. I am not a procurer."

Dzhaba lifted a hand in a wave. He would get his own women, thank you.

Georgi led them into the room he used as a war room and went over his plan with the two men from Georgia. His plan was simple. Put up strong defenses to defend his missiles and aircraft, then send the rest of the world an ultimatum. That ultimatum would be to return the Red Party and Red

Army to power or suffer the consequences. The traitors of the Soviets, those mongrels from Poland and Hungary, would be the first to pay tribute to the People's Army. If they failed to show their accommodation, then they would receive the first of the Red Army's nuclear warheads directly on their capitol cities.

The three men spent the rest of the day huddled with others who came and went to fill them in on the situation.

There was noise outside in the evening glow of the setting sun. Two men were being kicked along by five men in field uniforms with weapons. The two men were dressed in the traditional garb of local farmers. The armed men spoke in Russian.

"Move faster, dog!" a man shouted and kicked one of the men to a faster pace.

The men moved to the front of the headquarters where Georgi stood waiting. The two prisoners were forced to kneel and await a decision as to their fate.

A sergeant walked up to Georgi and saluted. He reported, "Comrade Leader, these two, they were found near our outer perimeter. I bring them here for interrogation."

From the bloody faces and skinned heads, they had already received a rough field interrogation.

Georgi walked up to the men and looked down on their bloody faces in the murky light of dusk. He asked, "Who are you?"

The older man raised his clasped hands to his face and cried, "We are Arshile and Aram! Poor shepherds, oh great sir. We have done nothing wrong. We know nothing about you."

"The two A's, eh," laughed Pyotr when he heard the men's names. He walked up beside Georgi. He smelled blood.

"Do you wish to question them?" Georgi asked Pyotr.

"Ah, it would be a pleasure to interrogate these two men. A man gets rusty without practice," the Don Cossack laughed. "Of course, there might not be much sleep for all tonight. Not if these men have strength. And they look strong. Men of the outdoors. Of the mountains. I just hope sleeping with sheep has not weakened them."

The guards joined in the laughter.

Well, someone is happy, thought Georgi. These people meant nothing to him. He said with a wry smile, "Enjoy yourself, my friend."

"They are good Armenian Christians. I will give them a head start to their god, or to their hell if that is their destination," Pyotr shouted in good humor. He walked off, motioning the sergeant to follow him with his prisoners.

I suppose I asked for this, thought Georgi, knowing of the racket Pyotr always caused. Oh, well, it will be better than this mountain silence.

The wails of men in agony went on through the night. The screams rose to a death pitch then suddenly dropped off to complete silence when the man passed out from pain. He would lay still like a stunned ox until he was roused again with a dash of cold water. He was then forced to observe his comrade being tortured until that one could stand it no longer and lost consciousness from sheer pain.

All Pyotr learned from these two hapless men was that the two men were father-in-law and son-in-law. They herded sheep for what was once a collective farm, but most of it was now owned by a man who had been the local party leader. They knew of nothing of the goings-on in the mountains. They had seen many men and heard noises of many vehicles, some that sounded like tanks, but they knew not what it was all about. They were simple shepherds who cared nothing for the doings of bigger, more powerful men.

They died two hours before dawn.

Pyotr looked down at the two men and shrugged his shoulders. He said, "Well, they kept me occupied for the evening. And I must say with admiration, they were both very strong men."

Pyotr believed in strength and power. Power ruled all things. He would make these local people feel his power, and from that power, these ignorant masses would tremble in fear. Trembling men were easy to rule.

He left the remains of the two prisoners behind to be taken care of by the sergeant and walked to headquarters. The sergeant on duty poured the Don Cossack a cup of thick, sweet Turkish coffee. Pyotr sat and sipped his coffee, waiting for the sun to come up so he could make his report to Georgi.

Ismet Kemal of the House of Omet looked west, to the mountains, wondering what was taking place in an area so near his home and lands. His men had seen men in uniform with tanks in the valleys at the foot of the mountains. Trucks pulled artillery pieces and loads of ammunition. The predominant markings were those of the Red Army of the Soviets.

A sharp, barking growl came from behind his gray beard. He thought the world had been rid of the Red Army and everything Soviet. Now there was a Red Army in the mountains where his people cut beech, oak and pine from the forest. There were also lush meadows they used in the summer to graze sheep.

Ismet Kemal was an Azerbaidzhan Turk, and his people had been in this region for over five hundred years. The House of Omet had been powerful in southwest Azerbaidzhan when the Turks controlled the country. His family had influence in the Ottoman Empire, and many warriors from the family had fought the Empire's wars. His family had opted for Turkish control over Iranian, and had lived under a brother Moslem country's rule without much difficulty. He was an Azerbaidzhan, but he was a Moslem first above all things. He had refused to Russianize his name, and he had paid for it. He had refused to pay tribute to the underling Communist Azerbaidzhan local government, and he had paid a price. The State had taken all of the land his family had held for over ten generations. The holdings had been vast and had supported his father's families and his father's brothers' families. Fifty other families who worked for the House of Omet had lived and prospered on the land. Then it had become a cooperative farm when Kemal was a young man in 1930.

When word came that the Soviet Union had dissolved and Azerbaidzhan was now a free country, Kemal gathered his twelve sons from his three wives, twenty-three grandsons and many other men of the family and rode around the old family holdings. They marked off the land that belonged to the old House of Omet and killed over one hundred men in the first two weeks. He posted a notice around the land that it belonged to his family and declared that all who were not off it in two weeks would meet the fate of the others.

The government in Baku had shouted loudly and sent a small force to deal with him. When the government force saw the size of Kemel's band, the commander told him he hoped that he would deal with the subjects in his area with righteousness and fairness. Kemal assured him that he was a good Moslem and the Koran had always been his guide in life.

"Father, do you worry about the army in the mountains?" asked Ismal, his son.

"The Red Army is no longer, so Moscow and Baku keep

telling us," Kemal told his son. "I wonder what they do there in our mountains to the west."

"I will send one of my sons and some men to find out," Ismal told his father.

"They must be careful, my son. It would be bad for our Islamic sons and brothers to be caught by such heathens," Kemal reminded him.

"I will send the hunter of the family. He is a woodsman and a mountainman. He will do well," Ismal said proudly.

"Then let it be done," said Kemal, still looking at the mountains.

The mountains did not belong to his family. They could not claim the trees, the grass or the water flowing from those lofty peaks. But they could, and did, claim that no outsider could take one square foot of their mountain. Those who tried had died in the past. It would be so this time.

11

Truck wanted to use the same staging area in Turkey they had used during the Gulf War. He liked the Turks he had dealt with and their professionalism. But he had been convinced by Bragg to go to Poland first and then on to southern Russia. He objected to going to Poland, knowing that Poland would be heavily infiltrated by KGB agents. The team might be compromised as well as its operation. He finally agreed to go to Poland. The team would be in Poland only long enough to link up with ground forces and move to a staging area just north of the Caucasus Mountains in southern Russia.

He wondered who all knew about this plan. Dan insisted that only a few men in Poland, Hungary and Russia knew of their mission. He hoped so.

"Truck, Colonel O'Neal and Captain Taborek have arrived," Crackers said as he stuck his head in from the outer office.

"Glad they made it," said Truck. He walked to the door to meet the two SF officers.

Lieutenant Colonel Gerald O'Neal was the Special Forces battalion commander for the Southern European Area Command. Captain Omar Taborek was an A-team commander. Both men had worked with the Eagle Attack Team during the Gulf War.

"Howdy, gentlemen. Welcome to the Eagle's Nest and Texas," greeted Truck.

"Glad to see you Colonel," returned O'Neal.

"Colonel," said Omar with a shake of Truck's hand.

They immediately got down to business. The two SF men would be in the States for only a short while, then they would go directly back to Italy and Turkey.

"Do we have any idea what the hell is going on inside Azerbaidzhan?" asked Truck.

O'Neal looked at Omar.

Omar spread his hands and said, "I got a rumor that an old Azerbaidzhan Turk family took back their old family holdings by force. Tough old bird made the Baku government stand down. Also a rumor came out of the Azerbaidzhan mountains that an armed force is being deployed into the area. This armed force has the markings of the Red Army, and they have both artillery and tanks. No aircraft have been seen except for normal helicopter supply and transportation. There is also a rumor that this old Turk family leader is very interested in what is going on in the mountains near his home. Word has been brought into Turkey that he is keeping the mountains covered with patrols."

"Can you learn more before we get there?" asked Truck.

"I've already sent in two men to make contact with this family," Omar informed him. "Both men are Turkish-born and damned outstanding SF men. They are both senior sergeants. If anyone can learn what is going on and set up good contact, these are the two to do it.''

"When can we make this man a major?" Truck asked O'Neal.

"Can you believe it, he hates the day he'll have to leave an A-team," O'Neal said.

"I can understand it," said Truck. Then he asked O'Neal, "Are your men meeting us in Poland?"

"Some will. The rest are slowly infiltrating into southern Russia,'' the colonel informed him.

That meant the men were probably HALOing in a team or section at a time. Truck had gone that route many times.

O'Neal continued, "They'll assemble on call when we have a launching site. No one, including me, knows where that site will be. Everyone knows only that the call will come suddenly and immediate reaction is required.''

"Tell your people to look out for armor. If they run into an armor unit of any size, don't take it on, call us. We've got a tank-stopping ability that's second to none," Truck told the two officers.

"We'll take some anti-armor stuff along just in case, but we'll call on you guys if anything big comes down the valley,'' promised O'Neal.

"The main things we're after are the nuclear warheads, and secondarily, destroying those missiles. If we can do that, we've done our job," said Truck.

"I think we'll be able to do just that," promised Omar. "I hope my two men can get a fix on those missiles. I'm counting on that. The warheads should be near by if we can find the missiles.''

That was the big worry to Truck, locating the exact area where those warheads were kept. As long as the Red Army had a nuclear capability, those warheads were a threat to the rest of the world. Maybe they would get some hard information on where the devices were located. This was where trusting in luck came in.

"We're gonna make this operation short and to the point, just like in the Gulf," Truck told them. "We're not going there to kick that bunch into submission. We're going to neutralize their nuclear capability and then out we go. The governments in the area can handle the rest of the problem without us. Hell! It'll give 'em something to do to forget about being hungry."

The other two men smiled. This old warrior had little feeling for the people of the old Soviet Union. Those people were still his enemy and would be until they proved otherwise. The people of Russia had stuck with a government that had the imperial objective of subjugating many small neighboring countries. Russia started out by engulfing the helpless republics around her borders. The next victims were war-torn Eastern European countries that could not defend themselves after World War II. The Red Party had made the Russian people believe that they were the best in everything and would one day rule the world. The people fell for it, having no compassion for the small countries they dominated, thinking only of their own power. No, Truck Grundy had no sorrow for their hunger or suffering this winter. He had buried too many friends because of the imperialism of the Soviet Union.

Truck told O'Neal, "I want to send Stu and Willie back with you. Let them hook up with the proper people in Poland. And look, they have a couple of radios that have not even been thought of yet, let alone invented."

"If we can't get them back alive, the radios will make it," Omar promised with a smile.

"Then let's send 'em along," agreed Truck. He yelled toward the door, "Crackers, are Stu and Willie standing by?"

"Got 'em, boss," Crackers replied and went to the door to call into the hangar.

When Stu and Willie arrived, the men went into a detailed study of the operation plan for the attack. O'Neal and Omar listened intently. When the plan was finished, they added their opinions on how to improve it with the new information they brought with them. Stu made additions and corrections as they talked.

Everything was in order. These men were professionals and knew that things changed with time. They were ready to add or subtract from the plan on a moment's notice. They were sure many things would change before they arrived in the Russian Caucasus.

Truck took O'Neal and Omar out for a big Texas steak before they got on their plane back to Bragg and then on to Europe.

O'Neal promised that the Polish and Russian ground troops would have SF people along. The operation would be kept secret until all of the forces were at the launch site.

Omar promised he would have made contact with the Turk family in Azerbaidzhan before the team arrived and feed the information he received to Truck.

Truck ate in peace. Things would take care of themselves or things would be screwed up as hell. A man could do only what he could do. The rest of the time he trusted to luck, good men, good experience and good planning.

"I don't know how many more operations are in the future for us professional soldiers," O'Neal said suddenly.

"At least you had Vietnam. Panama, the Gulf and things like this are all we younger soldiers can hope for," complained Omar.

"These young troopers don't have much of a soldier's life to look forward to," admitted O'Neal. "I'd sure hate to be coming on board right now and have nothing more to look forward to than these guys.''

God, I've heard that a lot lately, thought Truck.

Alex Mikolajczyk was recalled to Poland. Bela Metzger was recalled to Hungary. The U.S. news media stated, without fear of ever being contradicted, that there were strains forming between the United States and the two most progressive Eastern European countries, Poland and Hungary. Unnamed sources backed them up.

The President smiled when he saw the reports on TV.

When Truck saw the evening news as he was getting ready to board the C-5A air commando jet, he laughed like hell.

The Polish President's aide informed Alex that the President had not returned to the capitol, but the aide had been informed that the President must return for a national emergency. Alex was not sure the President or anyone else in Warsaw was aware of the threat hanging over their heads. When he saw them eye-to-eye and told them of the actions the United States was taking, they would believe.

Alex went to visit members of his family while he waited to see the President. He informed his family that there were no problems with the Americans and that no, he was not about to be canned by the Polish Government.

He ate sausage and homemade bread, washed down with good beer and enjoyed his grandchildren. These were the people who needed to be protected from the holocaust fomented by insane men. These young people were the future of Poland. They would live free from Communism and all the fear that system had instilled in its citizens. They would not have to lie in bed at night wondering if there would be a knock on the door because of something someone overheard them say. His people had come too far to now fear having nuclear warfare foisted upon them just as they were coming out of the yoke of Communism.

Our country must survive! The thought screamed in his mind.

It appeared to the family and all present that the Polish diplomat didn't have a worry in the world.

12

Ambassador Alex Mikolajczyk requested an individual audience with the President. The Polish President honored Alex's request. When the President learned of the military support the United States was going to provide, he knew for sure that the reports about the Red Army were serious. He called for the Defense Minister, General Stanislaw Peroski, and the commander for the Polish commandos, Colonel Hetman Beszczynski.

To Alex's surprise, all three agreed with him completely that they must work with the Americans to counter this threat. But they were worried about sending Polish troops onto Russian and Azerbaidzhan soil.

Alex gave them good reason why they should when he asked, "Who do we trust to do this job, the Russians?"

Nationalistic pride caused the chest of the President to puff up. The same pride was echoed by the two military men.

"We will defend out right to exist against all. We thank

the Americans for their help, but we will speak for Poland,''
the President said stiffly.

''To the death,'' announced Peroski.

The Polish Commando Commander was ordered to work
with the Americans and give them anything they wanted.
This was no time to argue about who should be in charge.
Work together.

Alex informed them that two Americans were on their
way and would arrive by airplane. The Americans would
also send their Special Forces people as a liaison with Polish
troops. In addition, a special unit would arrive that was
capable of neutralizing any armor the Red Army might
have.

The two military men looked up. The Minister said,
''That sounds like a unit that was used in Bavaria against
the neo-Nazis several months back.''

If that was the case, they knew the tanks would be taken
out quickly and professionally.

The Polish Government decided to use the secret airfield
the Soviets had built a few kilometers south of Warsaw. The
commando commander was ordered to meet the two Americans who were arriving and assist them in setting up a joint
military operation.

Colonel Hetman Beszczynski was waiting when Stu and
Willie arrived. He and his executive officer, Lieutenant
Colonel Klemens Takarzewski, took the two Americans to
a secure part of the airfield where a unit of two thousand
men had been quartered for the duration.

The Hungarian government promised the joint expedition
that it would send troops if requested. If the men were not
immediately needed, Hungary was ready to maintain a
standing reserve for her allies to call upon. Two Hungarian
army officers arrived as liaison officers for their forces.

The Polish commandos were quick to grasp the operation plan. The Soviet Government had been preparing its forces for war with Europe and the United States ever since World War II had ended. Now they were going to fight against the Red Army. Some of the older men in the commandos who had lived through the Soviet occupation of Poland gave wry grins when they learned of their mission. Maybe they would get some of the sons of those occupiers in their rifle sights. The Americans quickly found that there was no love lost between Poles and Russians.

The Poles divided their unit into four groups of five hundred men each. These task forces were to attack targets as directed and protect the nuclear experts who would go in with them and make sure all nuclear devices were retrieved. The men were to kill as many of the enemy as they could during the attacks. But this was not expected to be a long, sustained battle, and there was no ground to gain or hold for any length of time. They were to hit quickly, dominate their objectives and withdraw upon completion of their mission. The action was a typical commando operation.

After the plans were formulated, all they could do was wait. Waiting was a military condition all army men were experts at.

Stu and Willie enjoyed the Polish beer and sausage. Willie was a black man and as such was a novelty to the Poles. Willie was used to being in parts of the world where he was the only black man present. He smiled when he remembered his tours in Laos when he was in a group of Hmong tribesmen. Not only did he stand head and shoulders above all of them, his skin was a shade darker. The Viet Cong and North Vietnamese regulars called him the "Black Devil," which, to his mind, honored him greatly.

Both Americans enjoyed the company of the Poles, but

they wanted the action to start. They were easily bored with too much leisure time.

Sergeant First Class Frank "Bug Eye" Daglarie, US SF, and Sergeant First Class William "Handlebar" Selma, US SF, crouched in the shallow ditch. Daglarie meant "mountain" in the Turkish language. Daglarie and his entire family personified the mountain physique. They were big chested, broad shouldered people who were as strong as they looked. Selma was a small, wiry man with muscles that were stringy and as strong as woven steel. Both men had the dark complexions of their Turkish ancestors, and in civilian clothes, they looked much like any other citizen of that region. At present, they wore the traditional clothes of the Azerbaidzhan people.

They watched from cover as three men rode up on horseback. The men were traveling away from the mountains. They were Moslem Azerbaidzhan horseman from their dress and horse tack. Prayer mats of the faithful were tied to the backs of their saddles. The sun was now only one and a half hours old.

Daglarie looked at Selma and nodded. Selma returned the gesture.

Daglarie stepped up out of the ditch and onto the trail. He raised both hands, palms outward, to show that he was not carrying a weapon. He spoke in Turkish and said, "Peace be with you, brothers and believers in the true God."

The men pulled up their horses to stare at the two strangers. The leader asked, "Who are you."

"We are immigrant believers in the Koran and wish to take refuge with a true believer," Daglarie informed him.

The leader looked from one to the other. He sat his horse easily, as a man used to a saddle between his legs. "Your accent would make you Turks from the old country."

"That we are. And, kind sir, would you please lead us to your headman?" asked Daglarie.

"Can the other man speak as well?" asked the leader of the horsemen.

"I can speak, young sir, for I am also a Turk by birth," Selma informed him.

"Good. Jump up behind my two men. We have three hours to ride," the leader informed them. He started out, not looking back at the others.

Daglarie and Selma ran to the horsemen and jumped up behind them. The two horsemen kicked their horses to catch up with the younger man. The Americans noticed that the men held their mounts back so not to get ahead of the younger man. He was the leader. From the richness of his clothes, he was from a powerful family. Maybe he was a member of the family they were trying to contact.

Both of the Americans noticed that the leader spoke in a very old accent, indicating he was descended from Turkish people who had been isolated from Turkey proper for many years. Weren't the people they sought an old Azerbaidzhan Turk family?

The younger man led them to the gate of a large villa located at the end of a long drive. Tall trees lined the road leading to the grand house. He turned to the four men on the two horses and said, "My headman is my father. We are of the House of Omet. Tell me who you are before we go farther."

As he was talking, the two SF troopers were being forced off the horses to the ground.

Daglarie spoke slowly and with purpose. "We are now members of an elite American Army unit. We have come because of the military forces in the mountains."

There was surprise on the younger man's face for a moment, then he asked, "Are you not Turks?"

"Yes. We are also Americans. We are now American fighting men and we owe our allegiance to the United States and our unit."

These Azerbaidzhan men understood allegiance. Without loyalty to a person or a nation, a man did not belong to anyone but himself. Such a man was not to be trusted with another's life and property.

"I have been three days in the mountains. I was relieved this morning an hour before sunrise," the leader told them.

The two Americans stood and waited. They were at the mercy of others.

"I am the first-born of my father's third wife. He calls me Ata," the younger man told them.

"Ah, Ata, 'Chief,'" said Selma.

"Yes, that is so. My father tells me I remind him of his old grandfather," Ata said. He sat his horse a moment and then said, "Follow me."

Ata turned his horse down the lane and rode off. The other two horsemen laughed and turned their horses to continue to their homes in another part of the vast holdings of the House of Omet.

Daglarie shrugged his shoulders and started off in a trot behind Ata. A little run never hurt a true Special Forces trooper. In fact, it did him good and made him stronger.

Selma fell in beside him, his cloth pack flopping against his back.

The old one, Ismet Kemal of the House of Omet, stood and listened to the two Americans. He had never seen Americans before, even if they were Turkish-born. His dark eyes were bright and intelligent. When the two Americans spoke of the army in the mountains, the old man's eyes brightened with the look of a warrior.

Damned if he's not ready to fight, thought Daglarie.

Kemal had twenty-three men, running in two's and three's, to patrol the mountains. They had reported that the troops in the mountains were of the Soviet Red Army and had both artillery and armor. They had seen only three missiles so far, but there might be more. The men in the so-called Red Army of the People wore old Soviet uniforms and were from various republics.

The old man showed the two SF men a map with different unit locations. The map was a masterpiece, accurate, beautifully colored and inscribed in the Arabic script of the old Turkic language that was called Osmanli.

"May we work with you and your people?" asked Daglarie.

The old man stood a moment, accepting a cup of hot Turkish coffee from a servant, before he answered. "What can we do for people such as you, a country who has everything?"

"Help us direct an attack on this outlaw army and give us military intelligence only your people can obtain," Daglarie told him simply and directly. He knew that was the only way to be with this man.

The old man's gray eyebrows shot upward, his only show of surprise since he had met the two Americans. "Ah, an attack on the mountains. Who, may I pray to God for an answer, is going to attack this godless bunch?"

"The military of the United States of America. There will be men from other countries, but we do not know which at the moment," said Daglarie.

"The army that won so greatly over the great Satan and pretender, Saddam? If that is so, then we will help," Kemal said slowly. He looked around at his sons who had gathered. "Ata, have you been in the saddle too long?"

"No, my father. One hour with my new wife and I will be vitalized anew," the young man bragged to his father.

Men laughed.

"Ha!" cried the old man, joining in the laughter. "One hour with a new wife and I could not climb into the saddle."

The men laughed in good humor. The two Americans looked at the old man and knew that a new wife would only whet the appetite of the old warrior. He would die in the saddle, urging everyone else on to new heights.

Kemal turned to his eldest son, Faruk, who was past his middle years. "Faruk here, my eldest—he will be in command of our men in the field. If you need anything, he is the one for you to contact."

The two Americans nodded their heads that they understood.

"Then it is done," said Kemal. He lifted his coffee cup for a toast. "To the warriors of old and new."

"May God, the Most Merciful and True One, praise us all," returned Selma.

The union was sealed. These two men were now a part of a group of men who would die to protect each other or give aid. The only thing they asked in return was for the two Americans to do the same. There was no doubt in the Azerbaidzhan Turks' minds about their two new brothers, for were they not men of Turkish heritage?

13

Daglarie watched Selma walk toward him, one of Ata's men in front and one in the rear. The two Azerbaidzhans were charged with seeing that the American remained alive and in good health. Two men were also assigned to Daglarie.

Selma pulled out a map and pointed to a location. It was the last area they had found that the Red Army had used as an encampment. Selma grinned, "That's five of 'em. I think we got 'em all."

"Good. I'll call it in when the time comes around," stated Daglarie.

"We need to get a fix on them warheads, Dag," said Selma.

"Yeah. We'll do what we can. These two possible locations will help," replied Daglarie.

"They ain't possible locations. They're the real thing. Ata said his boys counted eight containers with radioactive signs on them," Selma reminded him. "There were other containers like that at both locations. Heavy containers mean lead to protect the atmosphere from radioactive material.''

''You're probably right,'' agreed Daglarie. He lay back against the bank of a small ditch that ran beside the trail.

They relaxed and munched on a piece of almond and date bread. One man stood guard at all times.

After a period of time, Daglarie looked at his watch and took a small transceiver out of his pack. He took a second machine of about the same size that Selma carried and linked them together with a short connecting wire. The second machine was a miniaturized computer. The transmitter's range was eight miles, line of sight, but enough for their mission. He made sure there were no trees blocking his overhead line of sight.

One item included in the report was an administrative directive. Kemal committed his men to the fight against the Red Army in the mountains. The men would be in civilian clothes, but that would not indicate what side they were on. It had been decided that all indigenous personnel would wear a red scarf around their necks to designate that they were United States allies.

He checked to make sure the computer had all of the information he wanted to send. When he was satisfied, he pushed a button on the transmitter to signal a plane flying high overhead that he was ready to send. He received a signal to start the transmission. He punched the send button, and the small computer fed the signal into the transmitter in short, twenty-character bursts to be broadcast over the air. In a matter of two minutes, the entire transmission was sent. After the information was taken back to base and typed into hard copy, the message would be ten pages long.

''Modern times and modern toys. They sure got us in a box, don't they?'' Selma asked Daglarie.

''How's that?''

"Well, look at this little thing," directed Selma. He looked the machines over with dark brown eyes, not sure he was happy with what he was seeing. "Everything is getting so small, and everything knows what everything else and everyone else is doing or not doing—pretty soon we won't be able to do a damned thing on our own."

Selma was a natural hater of anything mechanistic or modern. He would fare better in life if he stayed here in Azerbaidzhan with these people of the earth. But he was also caught up in his job as a Green Beret and would not willingly leave that profession, although he was tempted. The idea of being in a country like Azerbaidzhan that allowed a man to have four wives was tempting to a young man in his prime. Of course, that little American wife of his might not go along with the extra wives. But what the hell! His American wife wouldn't go along with being in Azerbaidzhan to begin with.

"I thought you were eyeing that big-titted woman kind of close," said Daglarie with a smile.

"Her name's Mubeccel. I think she could grow some fine kids," said Selma.

"I know they'd never go hungry," smiled Daglarie. "She'd be able to feed a small squad of her own with those big things."

"Ya know, I think I could handle two wives," said Selma, deep in thought.

Daglarie laughed. "You've been an American too long. You were only ten years old when ya left Turkey. Are ya sure ya got the mentality for it over here?"

"That's the problem: I don't know," admitted Selma.

Both men wondered about their ability to come back to a life such as this and fit in. Their worry was not only to fit in, but be able to live a full life under such strict living conditions, both religiously and materially. To live under the laws of the Koran took a dedication that the ordinary American didn't possess. Neither of the men had prayed five times a day in years. Not only had they stopped praying that often as boys, now that they were soldiers, warriors, Moslem laws did not require them to follow such a strict rule of prayer. Other laws were relaxed for a soldier.

Selma had refused to join Daglarie in eating bacon and sausage for breakfast. He remembered eating pork only once in his life when he was young. The thought of what he had done had made him sick to his stomach, and he had thrown up for two days.

Daglarie had been only a small boy when his family left Turkey, but he remembered the small, dusty village they lived in. His father had owned the largest store in the village. He realized now that it was a small hole in the wall compared to what his father now owned in the United States. And that was just a small store that both his father and his mother had to run because they could not afford to hire help. Daglarie wasn't sure he could adjust to life as these people lived it.

"Things should happen soon," commented Daglarie. He spoke in Turkish.

"I am ready to meet God, if it is to be. I am also ready to be a victorious soldier, if that is to be," replied Selma. He was more of a true Turk warrior than he realized.

The men with him agreed.

Vladimir Bokey stepped out of the small mountain cabin that was his headquarters. He had arrived from Moscow during the night. He watched the late winter sun rise over the vast steppes stretched below him. Ribbons of fog rose up along the paths of small streams of run-off snow in the mountains. The trees that covered the mountainsides were beech, oak and pine. The mountain grass was brown at the moment, but soon it would revive with the beautiful new green of spring. The countryside here was vastly different to the city man from Moscow from what he was used to. If he had been of a different mindset, he would have enjoyed that difference.

Not all of the Soviet generals had ignored his call to form a new government and army. Two of the best tacticians and strategists in the Red Army had agreed to join him. One of them had drawn up the plans for his entire encampment and its defenses. A navy admiral had promised to bring a sizable number of ships and submarines with him when he came over. The admiral's plans called for seizing ships with a nuclear capability at a later date. Some of those ships and submarines would come from the Black Sea fleet, which would send a strong signal to Ukraine that they were not giving any republic anything that belonged to the Soviet Union.

The two generals had not joined him in the mountains because their absence from Moscow would cause too much notice. Moscow was already a den of intrigue and rumors of more intrigue. Everyone was looking under beds and behind doors for coups against the new governments of Russia and the rest of the republics.

Vladimir Bokey thought there were too many investigative news reporters from the rest of the world in his country and it angered him. He had no use for the free press. They stuck their noses where they had no business. They reported on things they knew nothing about. When he and his party took control, such things as the free press, among others, would be changed.

From where he stood he could see the locations of the tanks that had been set up around his headquarters. Most of them were mainline T-72s with their huge 125mm main guns. To his north in a small, long valley were five missiles of a new design called the SSX-25. Only seven of these experimental missiles had been built, and two of them had been destroyed when the Soviet Union collapsed. Georgi Krasnov had spirited the other five away and documented them as being destroyed. The SSX-25 was to have been the weapon that the United States would fear because they would have nothing that could shoot it down. The missile was designed to fly higher and faster than anything in any known arsenal. But that was before the Gulf War and the U.S. Patriot missile had shown up. No one would have believed that one missile could actually shoot another missile out of the air. That was like shooting a bullet at another bullet and hitting it. When Georgi heard the reports of the U.S. Patriot, he had said it wouldn't be long before the United States would develop an anti-missile weapon that would be able to counter the SSX-25.

Other SS missiles were located in secret places. Three of those locations also had a nuclear capability.

A field vehicle groaned down the narrow mountain trail and stopped in front of the cabin. Vladimir stood and waited for Georgi Krasnov to reach him before he greeted the colonel. "So, Georgi, you are up early!"

"I haven't been to bed," said Georgi.

"Oh. What is wrong, Comrade?" asked Vladimir.

"My patrols have found tracks around these mountains. The patterns indicate that these people are scouting out the area, our area!" announced Georgi.

"Who?" was Vladimir's one-word question.

"We cannot catch any of these men. But we believe they are locals. Maybe they're only curious. I don't like curious men. They can kill you as dead as one of evil intent," said Georgi. "I will find these men, even if I have to search every hut and hamlet in the area."

Vladimir held up a hand to the colonel. He said, "Hold, Georgi. Let's not get carried away and start harassing the locals. We need their good will to remain in this region without always having to look over our shoulder. We won't have time to be fighting on our home front while we prosecute our plan.''

Georgi stood a moment, wanting to tell Vladimir to tend to politics while he tended to the military end of their business. But he knew the civilian was right. ''All right. I'll send out patrols to find out where these men come from. Later, when the time is right, then I will take care of this local problem.''

''Good. Come. We'll get a good cup of the strong Turkish coffee. That will help open your eyes from your lack of sleep.'' Vladimir led Georgi to the small hut that served as the cooking and eating facility for the headquarters.

Georgi would take time to drink coffee with Vladimir. He would smile and wish Vladimir a long life. But deep down, Georgi knew that he and his two brother army officers, the two generals that Vladimir was counting on, would take over and run the new Soviet Union as it should be.

Vladimir returned Georgi's smile, sure that he had an ally that he could count on.

Selma looked up when the man touched his arm. He looked in the direction the man was pointing.

Three men in the field uniforms of the Red Army's *spetsnaz*, the Soviet's answer to the Special Forces, walked along a narrow trail, following horse prints left by the Americans and Azerbaidzhans. The Red soldiers carried their entrenching tools on their belts, ready to be used as weapons in close hand-to-hand combat. They had red tabs sewn on both collars of their jackets and paratrooper insignias sewn above the right chest pocket, the designation of the *spetsnaz*.

Daglarie raised up high enough to see the men coming down a small rise at a distance of one hundred meters. He dropped back down behind the small berm they were behind and pulled out his large bowie knife. He indicated that this was what they would use to kill these three men. No shots would be fired. Selma nodded in agreement. Two of the Azerbaidzhan horsemen nodded in agreement and pulled out their long-bladed knives.

Daglarie motioned two other men to go to the horses and keep them quiet. The men slipped off to do it. A second Azerbaidzhan joined the three men lying hidden beside the trail. They would attack the men from the enemy's right side. From where they lay, they were no more than six feet from the middle of the trail.

The three Red soldiers neared the spot where the four men lay waiting. They came in a row, one at a time, one behind the other.

When they drew up even with the men lying in ambush, the four men sprang up from their hiding places and rushed the three enemy soldiers.

Daglarie ran into his *spetsnaz* target and stuck the blade of his knife deep into the man's chest. The blade was long, but it could not reach across the chest of the big Russian and slice his heart. The man gasped and struggled to free himself. Daglarie hung on and threw the man to the ground. He jerked out his knife and started to stab again, but he held back. This man needed to be questioned. He flipped the knife, caught it by the blade and swung hard to hit the Russian in the head with the handle. The man lapsed into unconsciousness.

Selma jumped out onto the trail and landed behind his target. He jumped on the back of the man and grabbed him around the neck from behind. He forced his arm up under the man's jaw and pulled his head backward. At the same time, the American pulled the sharp blade of his knife across the man's neck and killed him.

The two Azerbaidzhan horsemen ran to the Russian in the lead, one hitting him low with his knife and the other hitting him high. One man cut the legs out from under him while the other man nearly sliced the enemy's head off.

The fight was over quickly. These men were professionals at killing and butchering. The two Americans were professional soldiers and were trained in the art of killing, and the two horsemen were hunters and stockmen, used to butchering animals.

The two Americans and an Azerbaidzhan drug the Russians off the trail while the fourth man cleaned the trail to eliminate any appearance of a struggle.

A bubble of blood formed in a nostril of the wounded man. It popped, leaving a red ring of blood from the tip of his nose to the top of his mustache. None of the warriors cared if the man died, but they did want him to remain alive until they could interrogate him.

"He's got a sucking chest wound, Selma. I gotta fix him up, or he ain't gonna make it," said Daglarie.

The big Turkish American cut open the man's jacket and placed a plastic patch over the wound. He taped it tight. He gave the man a shot of Demerol to ease his pain and help keep him alive. The communications equipment and a few medical supplies were the only American-made articles the two men had brought with them. They carried AK-47s like their comrades.

"Ya know, we don't have a lot of that shit if we get into a fight and need it for ourselves," Selma reminded him.

"Gotta figure the priorities, my man. Mine right now is to keep this pig-fucker alive," Daglarie announced. "So let's get him back to the ranch."

They placed the wounded man over the saddle of a

horse, and one of the Azerbaidzhans climbed up behind the saddle. They rode off to the headquarters of the House of Omet. The old man would know what to do with the Russian. All the two Americans wanted out of him was information as to who he was and how many of them there were in the mountains. The two men were sure that their new friends would know how to extract any information this man had locked away in his brain.

14

The two United States Air Force C-5As and the C-130 flew to the secret airfield the Soviets had built not far from Warsaw, Poland. This was the first armed force of the United States military to enter Poland since World War II.

Truck watched the lights of the capitol city to the north. He was glad they were going to an isolated airfield outside the hustle and bustle of a large population complex. They would land, the men would disembark from the aircraft and go into a hangar that would be provided for them. The U.S. aircraft would remain isolated from the rest of the facility and be closely guarded. No one except the aircraft crew or members of the Eagle Attack Team would be allowed near the airplanes. Orders had been given to shoot unauthorized persons who tried to get to the aircraft.

The large, droop-winged C-5A made a soft landing on the field and taxied to its designated place. It was followed by the second C-5A and the C-130.

The crewmen opened up the personnel doors on the

aircraft to let the passengers out. They remained behind to do after-flight checks and get the aircraft ready for takeoff.

Buses met the Americans and took them to the large hangar that was to be their home for the next few hours. Inside were cots, tables and a place to eat. Coffee, pastries and other foodstuffs awaited them on a long table. The men were grateful for the thoughtfulness of their host country.

Matt Helm walked to where Truck was standing. Truck was never surprised when this man showed up. Matt said, "I've got the proper Polish military people for you to talk with."

He turned and Truck walked with him to a door at the rear of the hangar. He opened the door and entered. Truck followed him inside and they found three men dressed in civilian clothes. Matt introduced them as Generals Stanislaw Peroski and Ion Myszka and Colonel Hetman Beszczynski. General Peroski was from the Polish high command and was authorized to approve any and all military involvement. General Myszka was the commander of operations. Colonel Beszczynski, who would be with the ground troops, was the commander of the Polish commandos and Truck's link to the Polish Government. Truck would be introduced to the Russian military commanders when he reached the Caucasus.

Ukraine had given its approval for overflight of its territory by the combined military forces. The Ukranians were not given direct access to the military action, but they were made aware of the threat the outlaw Red Army of the People posed to their country as well as the rest of the world. Truck wasn't really worried about the political and international interactions of nations. All he wanted and needed was access to the battlefield.

Stu, Willie and O'Neal were called into the room, and they quickly went over their plans, which were simple. The plans had also received tentative agreement from the Russians.

The Eagle Attack Team, using the night capability that the TORCH system gave it, would attack and destroy the enemy's armor capability and fly armed cover for the ground forces. The ground forces would locate and destroy all missiles found, and a team trained in nuclear weapons would recover the warheads. The Poles would attack two of the five encampments of the Red Army and the Russians would attack the remaining three. A spy in the Red Army had given Russian intelligence operatives (the old GPU) locations of most of the nuclear warheads.

The plan was simple and it was dangerous. The Poles and Russian military planned to set down in the middle of the camps and shoot it out. There were no real military tactics involved. The attacking force was there only to pin down the enemy to keep him from reenforcing other encampments. The main thrust of the battle was to get men to the nuclear warheads and destroy the missiles. Time and the size of the Russian Army would counter any threat the outlaw army wished to heap upon its fellow countrymen. The Russians believed that once the nuclear capability was neutralized, the Red Army of the People would disband. Trials and executions of the leaders would dampen enthusiasm for any future rebellion.

Truck was satisfied that his people were not going to be sent into a meat grinder. O'Neal modified his peoples' advisory effort to keep them out of harm's way as much as possible. This was no time to completely refuse to join the attack. But he was damned sure he was going to keep track of his men, and if they were subjected to what he called ''outlandish military tactics,'' he was going to go to their rescue. O'Neal made it plain to the Polish commanders that if he called for Polish helicopter support, he had better get it. They agreed that he would have priority, not wanting to get any more Americans killed then was absolutely necessary.

The three Poles shook the Americans' hands and left the building. Matt followed them out, promising Truck to keep him informed of any changes, even the slightest ones.

After they were left alone, Truck looked at Stu. His eye switched to Willie and O'Neal. ''I reckon we can live with it or ya'll wouldn't have gone along.''

''You heard what I had to say,'' O'Neal said. ''I want to do the best we can. Hell, we're Forces people. We gotta be good. But I'm not going to put my men in a situation that'll get them killed because of bad planning or leadership.''

''I think we can do all right with the plan,'' said Stu. ''I'll be able to clean this thing up once we get to the Caucasus and link up with the Russians.''

''Stu, we don't take shit off the Russians. They don't have a thing we need except choppers to haul men, cannon fodder and a presence so we can go do what we have to,'' said Truck.

''I didn't think they'd get far with you along,'' grinned Stu.

''We're located with the Poles in the next hangar over,'' Willie informed Truck.

''Okay. Ya'll stay with it and call if ya need me and the boys,'' said Truck.

''That's a 'roger' on that,'' laughed Stu, glad that he would have the support of the team if it was needed.

The three Americans left to rejoin their Polish counterparts.

Truck called the team members together in the secure room and told them of the plan. They spent the next two hours discussing the operation. By the time they were through, he was comfortable with this phase of the mission. Next would be meeting with the Russians. He knew they would be hard to deal with. They would try to lord it over the Poles. Truck wouldn't take lording over from anyone, let alone from an ex-Communist army officer.

Five Polish Army women were behind the long table of food and drinks when Truck went back into the hangar. All five were young and not bad looking. Three of them were well endowed in the breast department. Team members hung around the five girls as if they had not seen a woman in months. The normal mentality of a soldier.

Crackers was trying to line the men up so everyone had a chance to visit with the women. He was hustled off by other team members.

Truck walked up to Red Dog and said, "The boys have got a diversion."

"Yeah. Anything with a pair of tits would divert this bunch," growled Red Dog.

Truck smiled. Red Dog was happy only when flying his Apache or drinking his Scotch and eating a half-raw steak.

"I talked to the Polish commanders of the operation," Truck told Red Dog. "We'll meet with the Russians on our next stop."

"I don't like dealing with no Russian," stated Red Dog matter-of-factly.

"Me neither," Truck agreed.

"Are we gonna have security for our forward people?" asked Red Dog. He was talking about the forward resupply teams the team used.

"The Poles said they would take them in and provide security for our forward people," Truck informed him. "They have a better map of the area so we can find where in the hell we are. The commando CO promised to send one over."

Red Dog nodded and finished the hot coffee provided him. He looked at the women again and motioned with a nod of his head to a tall, lanky woman. He said, "Now I'd crawl on that one's frame in a minute, if I had a chance. Man! Those long legs could wrap completely around ya."

Truck agreed with that. He walked over to the coffee pot and got a fresh cup of coffee. One of the girls smiled at him. Even they knew who held the power and rank by looking at him.

" 'Fraid you're younger than my daughter," Truck mumbled under his breath as he walked off.

Two of the girls went behind some equipment with Americans to be out of sight of the rest of the men. Money was a scarce commodity in Poland. All of them had families counting on them. Greenbacks were worth more than any other currency in any former Communist country. These Americans had that hard currency and were willing to part with it. For the Americans, they were not committed to anyone or anything. This was just a short sexual encounter before battle.

Truck took a copy of the operation plan and went into a corner to read over the changes that had been made. He was prepared to make and receive more changes as things began to develop. He didn't notice the men and women doing what men and women had been practicing since the first wars began.

They planned to leave in a few hours. That would put them on location before dark. They could unload and prepare their aircraft for battle. This would give their forward resupply people time to set up and be ready for them. They would attack before dawn. By this time tomorrow, they would be getting their equipment back on the airplanes and heading back to the States.

Truck used the rest of the time he had to go over in his mind the different Russian military phrases and markings on equipment and documents he had learned over the years. He wanted to make sure that he could remember Soviet markings for nuclear missiles.

He looked up and saw that Crackers was setting up his basketball net and calling everyone together for a last game. There was no indication from the men that they were hours away from a battle that might take their lives.

Who, me get killed? That's the other guy's worry, not mine! That was the attitude of most soldiers he knew. Why not? There was no need to worry about something you could not control. The route of a bullet or piece of an exploding artillery round was beyond any mortal man's control. Relax and take it easy, it may all turn out to be a dream.

The noise from the game of basketball brought Truck back to the present.

"Hey, boss!" Bad Bear yelled, interrupting his peace. The big Kiowa led an American Army officer toward Truck. The army colonel walked like a man of purpose. Truck saw an American Air Force officer not far behind, talking to some of the team members.

Truck stood up and waited for them to reach him. The air force officer walked over to join them.

"Truck, this is Colonel Reechling and Colonel Hainsworth," Bad Bear said to introduce the two men.

"I'm Louis and this is Bob," corrected Air Force Colonel Reechling.

"Gentlemen," greeted Truck, with a nod of his head.

"We are here to assist you in dealing with the Russians," said Bob, coming directly to the point.

Truck looked at him steadily for a moment. He wondered

who in the hell brought these two guys to this hangar. Truck also was always to the point. He told him, "I do my own dealing with people when I'm in an attack mode."

The army colonel started to say something, but Truck butt in with, "Who the hell brought you to this hangar, anyway?"

"The Poles told us you were here," Louis put in.

"Well, boys, turn your asses around and march right on outta here. This is a classified unit and a classified operation," Truck told them. "This is a need-to-know unit and you don't need to know."

"We're here to do a job," announced Louis.

"Either leave quietly, or I'll have you thrown out on your ass," Truck told Bob in a quiet voice.

Bob looked from Truck to Bad Bear.

Bad Bear shrugged his shoulders, "We ain't active military, Colonel. This old boy gives me an order to kick your ass and it gets kicked."

"We'll see about this when we get back to the States," growled Louis in a huff. He did an about face and left. Bob followed him out.

Bad Bear stood, watching in wonder at the two retreating men. He shook his head and asked, "What in the hell?"

"Another one of the problems of command," Truck told him. "I don't know where they come from, let alone why they were here."

"Let's get something to eat," suggested Bad Bear. "We should be leaving pretty soon."

The two men walked to the long table. A Polish male soldier was behind the table. There wasn't a Polish woman in sight.

15

The Eagle Attack Team loaded onto their assigned airplanes. Truck looked around at the helicopters and the fixed-wing 0-2 tied down in the big belly of the C-5A. The helicopters' rotor blades had been loosened and swept back for transport aboard the aircraft. It would not take long for the maintenance team to refit the choppers for flight when they arrived at their destination. Truck walked up the stairs to the passenger compartment. He sat down in a vacant row of seats. Being the leader allowed him seats all to himself.

Bad Bear sat across the aisle from him. The Kiowa warrior gave him a thumbs-up. The two were going off to another battle together. They had survived tours to Vietnam, Laos and other missions in many parts of the world together.

The crewmen of the C-5A cranked the engines, revved them up to operating RPM, kicked off the brakes and swung the huge aircraft out onto the service strip. The pilot fell in behind a Polish aircraft carrying the Polish commandos, the two Eagle Attack Team men and the men from the American SF.

On signal from the tower, the planes took off down the runway and became airborne. The lead craft turned southeast for their flight to adventure and another battle for the American team of professional warriors. The other aircraft followed in turn.

Truck looked around at his men. They were as relaxed as a college football team making a trip to a weekend game. He smiled. Professional was the word that entered his mind every time he thought about the members of his team.

They would fly to the southern part of Russia and meet a Russian force near the town of Makhachkala. While they were preparing the helicopters for flight, their forward support team, along with maintenance crews, would travel to the small border town of Akhty. Akhty was located in the mountains only a few miles north of the Azerbaidzhan border.

Lieutenant Colonel Donald Day, U.S. Air Force, Retired, walked past Truck's seat on his way to the coffee pot. He was one of the best observation pilots Truck had ever seen. He had been a member of the highly classified Raven Program in Laos during the war. The Ravens had flown their small single-engine O-1 Birddogs in some of the worst battlefield conditions during the entire war in Southeast Asia. Day had also flown many hours in South Vietnam. With such men making up the team, Truck knew he had the best.

Truck leaned back against the seat and relaxed. It was going to be a long night and an even longer day.

A servant girl came to Daglarie's room and told him that the Chief of the Omet house desired his presence.

Daglarie found Kemal in his favorite room. It was a

man's room, one where men could drink coffee, smoke, talk of the day's doings and plan things to come. This was the room where Kemal, as chief of the area, dealt out justice to wrongdoers and rewards to those found worthy.

He found Kemal sitting on a pillow, puffing on the long tube of a large *hookah*. There were three other tubes for other smokers of the water pipe. A bowl of tobacco glowed brightly each time the old man took a puff. He looked like some Mideast potentate dressed in a turban, loose fitting house pants and a colorful robe.

"Come, sit with me and smoke. We'll drink a cup of coffee and talk of things," invited Kemal.

Daglarie sat down on a pillow and picked up a tube from the *hookah*. He wasn't a smoker, but he would indulge this old man who he had come to respect in such a short time. He drew in a puff of smoke and blew it out. The smoke ran through the tubes that were cooled by water, and it was not as hot and biting as tobacco smoked in other forms.

"We must remember to praise Allah, God, the Beneficent King and Creator of the Universe, Who is Lord of the Three Worlds," said Kemal.

"He has been praised," returned Daglarie. "My father is of the old order, he prays to Allah, our Great Magnificence, the One and only True God, the God of Abraham, five times a day."

Kemal took another puff of smoke and inhaled deeply. He was glad these two Americans had come among them. He had learned that even those of the True Faith could pray to God in their own manner in the United States. One hears so many things about other peoples that it is difficult to know the reality of things. It was always a good thing to learn from those who know and not just from those who tell you what they hear.

"When do you think your people will attack?" asked Kemal.

"I received a message just before I returned to the house. Our people attack at zero-two-thirty hours," Daglarie told him. This man had a right to know, plus the sergeant trusted him as much as he did any fellow American.

"Ah, so it starts!" the old man breathed, wishing he were young enough to ride and fight as he did in the days of old. But the younger ones came, and the old ones were left behind with the memories of past glories and loves.

"I have told my people of you. They will stay out of the steppes and away from your people," said Daglarie. "Of course, we have no control over the enemy."

"If they come this way, then they will come," announced the old man, wise in the ways of warring men. "The rest is up to God, the Most Merciful and All Knowing."

All Daglarie could do was nod his head in agreement.

"My men will go with you," Kemal said and motioned toward the back of the house with his head, "and your friend. My men will do what they have to do to help in this battle. For this is an important battle to me and my people. To our entire country and way of life. I will not allow it to return to those heathen, godless Communists. Those people in our mountains are part of that world and a danger to us and the rest of the world."

Daglarie agreed. He didn't know all that was involved with this group in the mountains, but he did know that any force with a nuclear capability was not only a danger to Azerbaidzhan, but to everyone and everything on earth.

"A man should go to war with the picture of beautiful women left behind in his head," Kemal said with a laugh. "There is a place not far from here where women dance and a man can relax, to drink coffee and talk of good things. I have told my son, Fezi, to take you and your comrade there on this last night.'' The old man paused and said with a laugh of pleasure, ''That is if your comrade can tear himself away from my great-grand niece, Mubeccel.''

Daglarie smiled and agreed. ''He is enchanted, no doubt about it. I would be pleased to go.''

Kemal clapped his hands together and the servant girl appeared. He told her to go get Fezi and Selma.

Fezi entered the room and motioned for Daglarie to join him.

Daglarie stood up and bowed to Kemal.

Kemal rose to his feet and walked to Daglarie, his hand held out before him. Daglarie grasped it and Kemal said, ''When you leave my house, it may be forever, for you go from your place of pleasure to battle. If you live and have time, please return to visit with us. You will always find shelter in my home. May God, the Most Merciful and the True One, protect you and your friends.''

Daglarie bowed again and felt honored when he was embraced and kissed on both cheeks by Kemal. When a Moslem gave you the shelter of his home, that meant he would die to keep you from harm.

''Master, may the All-giving and All-merciful One be your guide to life and the hereafter,'' said Daglarie.

The old man exclaimed, ''*Alhamdolillah!*'' It was an old Arabic term for ''Praise be to Allah!''

The American left the old man standing in the middle of the room. He and Fezi walked down the hall to where Selma stood, placing food in his rucksack that the women of the kitchen had given him. Selma looked back longingly at the room he had just left as Daglarie lead him out of the house by the arm.

''I will return. I will return,'' promised Selma, speaking in Turkic. He looked at Daglarie. ''When we get back to

Turkey, I'm gonna put in for a leave and come back to this place.''

"They might not approve ya taking a leave here," said Daglarie.

"Fuck 'em if they don't, 'cause this is where I aim to come," said a determined Selma.

They got onto a truck with all their gear and eight other men. The truck driver drove off in a cloud of dust.

The truck pulled into a small hamlet of adobe structures just as the sun dropped below the horizon. There was one street through the heart of the village. Just after entering the hamlet, the driver pulled up to a large building and stopped. Mideastern-style music flowed out of the building. The sound of the music was part of the local culture to both of the Americans.

The men jumped out of the truck and went inside.

Ata greeted them and led them to a table that was reserved for the men of the House of Omet. It was a large round table near the dance floor. A woman was dancing when they entered, and she moved closer to the table when they were seated, her hips gyrating to the beat of the music. She was a belly dancer and danced for the pleasure of the men. She had been trained as a dancer since she was a small girl and knew her business well.

A waiter stood off to the side. The manager of the hall came forward in a hurry, for these were men of the most powerful family in the area. Besides, this man and everyone in the building owed Ismet Kemal nearly everything.

Ata informed the manager that they wanted a little of all the house had to offer. With a laugh, he included the women.

Waiters brought forth urns of sweet Turkish coffee,

meats, breads and cakes of every description. These were men going to war and they deserved the best.

Only Fezi, Ata and three other leaders knew the time of the upcoming battle.

The melody and beat of the music caught Daglarie's attention first. Then he watched a young belly dancer glide out onto the floor. He sat with his mouth open, stunned by what he saw. She was the most beautiful woman he had seen in his entire life. Her belly was firm and rounded with a fullness that made him want to run to her and kiss it. Her breasts were high and pert.

As her hips swayed in time with the music, her feet seemed to pull her closer to him. She had seen him when she first came onto the dance floor. He was the most handsome man she had ever seen. He was broad in the shoulders and had the build of a warrior. His face was handsome.

Selma saw the look on his friend's face. He waved a hand in front of Daglarie's face. The man paid no attention. Selma looked at Fezi and Ata and said with a smile, "You talk about a man struck dumb, this is he."

"Is not that a fact," said Fezi.

"I have heard of a man and a woman being struck with each other from first sight, but I do not remember ever seeing such a thing," said an amazed Ata.

Turhan, a nobleman and kinsman of the family, looked at Daglarie and then at Selma. He said, "This woman is my cousin. She is beautiful to behold, is that not true?"

"Ain't that for a fuckin' fact," breathed Daglarie in English.

The other men didn't know what he said, but they knew he was pleased with what he saw.

Turhan told Selma, "She is not only a woman of much beauty, she is also of good nature and taught in the ways of womanhood as a true Moslem."

"I'm sure my friend would be impressed," said Selma.

"If you can return after the trouble has passed, we will be glad to see you," said Turhan, speaking for the woman as one of the headmen of the family.

After the girl finished her dance, Turhan called her to the table. She stood, fearful of sitting at the table of such powerful men. Daglarie talked to her as she stood. He noticed her discomfort and bid her leave. The girl looked at Turhan, not wanting to offend him and his friends.

"Go, little one, and I will bring this man to you some day," said Turhan.

The girl left, bowing as she went.

Finally Daglarie said something they all knew, "That is one fine looking woman."

The evening continued with more dancing women and eating, but little else mattered to Daglarie than the sight of the beautiful dancing girl.

After a while, Fezi looked at his watch. He motioned that they should leave. The men left the hall and clambered onto the truck. Two more trucks were parked nearby. Men were loading onto those two trucks, ready to follow when the lead vehicle moved out.

"We will meet other trucks as we go," explained Ata.

The trucks neared the bottom of the mountains, the drivers driving with the lights off. The trucks stopped at proper intervals and men jumped from them to relieve men who had been at their posts all day.

The two Americans went with the two largest groups, each man going with the one to which he was assigned. They were given a man as a radio operator and another man to act as guard. For the Azerbaidzhan warriors it was both an honor and a fearful thing to be a bodyguard for such men.

Before Daglarie jumped off the truck to join his group, he

told Selma, "I'm coming back to this place. I don't give a damn if I've got to give up the Forces."

Then he disappeared into the dark.

I'd a never known it if ya hadn't told me, Selma thought, as he smiled in the night.

16

The planes started landing before dark. The airfield was small, so to make room for the incoming aircraft, arrangements had been made to move all Russian equipment to other airfields.

The Polish commandos off-loaded first. They were marched to an area provided for them. Truck noticed that they were kept well away from the Russian soldiers. He made a mental note of that.

Truck was sure that trouble would start as soon as the combined leaders began making final plans for the operation. Truck had spent a tour in Germany and had worked for a general who had to deal with the Soviet Military Liaison Mission. The Soviets were cool and smooth when dealing in public. But when they were behind the closed doors of a conference room, they became arrogant and demanding. They constantly harkened back to their defeat of Germany in World War II to bolster their current attitudes. Truck didn't figure their military strategy or tactics were worth two cents, and he knew they were lucky to have the United States on their side in the fight against Germany. In other words, Truck didn't have much use for his ex-Communist allies.

He turned his attention to the off-loading of his team. He would wait for a call for all leaders to meet.

General Ilich Lomonosov, the Russian commanding general for the operation, stood and watched the Polish soldiers exit the airplane. There was open hostility to Polish troops being on Russian soil, but the Moscow Government had approved the operation. Ilich knew he had the Americans to thank for that. He held all Poles in low regard. He didn't agree with the high praise General Anatoly Barchugov gave the Polish soldiers. Anatoly had spent too much time in Poland. He even had a Polish mistress he had brought back to Russia and installed in an apartment in Moscow.

Ilich growled to V.N. Ustinov, "We not only have the Americans, we also have those Poles to deal with."

"The problems of command," V.N. Ustinov told him lightly. He didn't care for either country himself. As Political Officer, he would put up a good front as long as he could. To Ustinov the old teachings of the Communist Party was hard to unlearn. He was alone on this operation at the insistence of Ilich, not of the government in Moscow, which still mistrusted former dogmatic Red Party Political Officers. And V.N. was, if not smart, dogmatic.

"Tell Anatoly that his pet Poles are here," Ilich told Major Lidiya Sverdlova, his aide-de-camp.

"Yes, General," she said and left to find Anatoly.

Ilich pointed and said, "There's the Americans with all of their fancy equipment, coming to save Mother Russia for us."

"Ah! We are supposed to be gracious and grateful, dear

Ilich,'' said V.N. in a bitter voice. ''I will be grateful and gracious—in public.''

''Your position is shaky with the government, so I understand. They may cut your pay off at any time if you do not toe the line. I am an old warrior and have funds in place for my retirement. I don't have to bow to those imperialists sitting in Moscow, or to these getting off these airplanes,'' Ilich told him.

''Ah, we're in a new day, Comrade. *We* are now imperialist.'' V.N. gave a wry laugh.

''Not me! Never!'' was all Ilich said. He raised his binoculars and looked at the man standing in front of the C-5A. ''That American has only one eye. I can see his black patch. So, the United States Government sends us pirates.''

V.N. smiled at that.

Lidiya had returned and was standing a respectful distance from the two leaders. Ilich told her, ''Send out word for all commanders to meet at once for a command briefing.''

She left to execute the order. She would give the order to the operations officer who would send out messengers to relay it to the various commanders.

''Do you know the commander of this renegade force we're after?'' asked V.N.

''Yes. He's Vladimir Bokey. I remember him as a promising young army officer, but he decided to leave the uniform and advance his status in the Party as a bureaucrat,'' replied Ilich.

''And do you know the two generals who may go with him?'' asked V.N.

''Yes,'' said Ilich, but he made no further comment.

''And the admiral?''

Ilich looked at V.N. Ustinov. He did not know. He said, ''Your connections with the KGB are showing, Ustinov.''

N.V. smiled.

"We must meet with these imperialists," said Ilich, and he walked off toward his operations building.

Truck brought Stu, Bad Bear, Red Dog and Willie to the meeting. Louis Reechling and Bob Hainsworth were also present, but both men kept their distance from Truck and his people. The Polish, led by General Ion Myszka, with Colonel Hetman Beszczynski and Lieutenant Colonel Klemens Takarzewski, were present. U.S. SF Lieutenant Colonel Gerald O'Neal and his executive officer, Major Philip Yelton, were with the Poles.

Ilich immediately determined that he was the ranking military person present and that the Americans had not even sent a general along. Ilich tried to ignore the presence of the Polish officers.

Truck smiled. Ion's face was blank, but Truck was sure that the Pole's guts were churning with anger.

"I have made a little plan to handle this small problem," Ilich announced.

Then he began to lay out an operation plan that was totally opposite to what the joint governments had approved when Truck was brought into the picture. This plan called for Truck and his team to be in reserve with the Polish commandos. The Russians would carry out the attack on the Red Army and search for any nuclear warheads. The attack would not take place until after twenty-four hours of preparation by air and artillery. While the air and artillery attacks were underway, a ground contingency force would move into the steppes on the eastern side of the mountains and drive out all civilians in the area. Then an attack would be made at dawn.

Truck kept his peace while the general talked through an interpreter. When the Russian general paused, Truck asked,

"Do you know where the nuclear warheads are located, General?"

"No, but they can be found," was Ilich's answer.

"I know where all of them are located. I know how to get to them. Your government and my government, along with the Poles, have approved my team to attack those three places. The Poles are to provide commandos to secure the areas after my team clears out defensive tanks and bunkers. The Russians are to provide nuclear experts and helicopters to transport the warheads out of Azerbaidzhan. The time of the attack was designated by the joint governments to be tomorrow at zero-two-thirty hours. In other words, tonight. The Azerbaidzhan Government has approved this arrangement, and we are in their country, not Russia. That's how my plans were drawn up. That's how I'm going to operate."

The general looked at the men before him. His eyes held death. He was a Russian general, one experienced in Angola and Afghanistan. No imperialist American was going to tell him how to make an attack upon any military force, particularly one he had trained and served with.

"Sir," requested Colonel Bob Hainsworth, "may I speak?"

"If you have any authority over these Americans," said Ilich.

"I suggest we get in contact with Moscow and Washington before we go any farther," suggested Bob. "We need to have better communications between us and set up better rapport."

"I believe you are right," V.N. Ustinov put in.

Truck's hackles rose. He wasn't going to sit here with his team while they lost both surprise and intelligence to the Red Army. This was supposed to be a quick strike and withdrawal. This was the reason he hesitated to work with outside units.

"I attack tomorrow morning as scheduled," announced Truck. "The Polish commandos are also ready. If we sit around here for a couple of days, the enemy will learn our location, who we are and will take measures to counter us. I won't lose men just so some bighead can make himself look good."

Bob broke in before anyone could say anything, trying to cut off any face-to-face confrontation between the Russians and the Americans, and said, "We are guests here, Mister Grundy. We must allow the general to provide the leadership in this operation without question."

"I am not a guest here. I was requested to come here by the joint governments of this operation, which includes Russia. The Poles and I will attack as scheduled," repeated Truck. "If the general thinks the governments of our countries and the public will favor his decision and condemn me, then so be it. But we won't be able to control the American and Polish press after this is over with. And I gaur-un-tee you that they will be well informed of what actions were taken here and who took them."

Ilich sputtered. He had never been opposed like this before. Who did this one-eyed American think he was, a cowboy? When he made decisions, then those decisions were followed to the letter. But he was not sure where he stood with the government in Moscow, or if they would back him like in the old days when the Red Party was in control. Neither he nor the government had control over the news media as they once had. Although there were no news people here at present, he was sure that Azerbaidzhan would allow any reporter from any country in to investigate once this mission was completed.

"Mister Grundy, if we fail, you will have to answer to me," was all Ilich could think of to say. He was trying to save face for being rebuked by a low-ranking American soldier. "Remember, you must go back through my country to get home."

"All I gotta do is call my aircraft anywhere in the world," Truck informed him. "Our aircraft can land in the nearest smooth spot they can find. Azerbaidzhan has many good places. Our friends in Turkey are not far away and I'm sure Armenia would let us use their airspace if needed."

Ilich looked at Truck with open hate. He turned to General Barchugov and ordered, "Anatoly, draw up a plan with these people for this mission."

"Yes, General," Anatoly said with a nod of his head.

General Barchugov requested Truck and his people and the Polish general and staff to join him in the war room. Anatoly and Ion knew each other well. Anatoly had been instrumental in the training of the Polish military. He knew their abilities.

The plan followed the guidelines as recommended by the combined governments. The only changes made were those caused by newly received military intelligence and changes in force structure.

Truck had one question. What was the status of the Azerbaidzhan Government?

Anatoly informed him that the Azerbaidzhan Government had agreed to let the combined force of Russian, American and Polish forces handle the problem in the mountains. The Azerbaidzhan Army would run patrols along the edges of the battlefield and stop any escaping Red Army soldiers.

Everyone was satisfied with that.

By the time Truck got back to the team, the team's aircraft had been checked out for combat, and the men were standing by, ready to get on with the job and away from Crackers's basketball.

Bad Bear walked up to Truck. "Hear that music, boss?"

A group of Russians were gathered across the airfield with a large fire burning and men dancing in a cleared circle.

"Yep. Russian. It's the music of the Cossack," answered Truck.

"A Russian captain invited us over to watch the dancing and drink a little vodka," Bad Bear informed him.

"Ya know how I am about drinking when shootin' is about to start," said Truck.

"I know, boss, but a little female companion and music ain't gonna hurt us," said Bad Bear.

"Okay, Bear. We'll go over that way for a while," agreed Truck. "But that Russian captain had better not let General Lomonosov find out she invited us."

Bad Bear led Truck and a few others to the meeting place the Russian captain had pointed out to him.

Captain Katya Kurakina smiled when the tall Kiowa walked up to her. She was in an army uniform with the crest of the new artillery corps. She wore a fury *shopka* with her regimental crest in the center of the turned-up bill. "Ah, the big American, who look so good." Her English was high school, but she could be understood.

"Yep. And I brought along a few friends," Bad Bear told her.

"Do you wish for to have vodka?" Katya asked.

"No. We don't drink on duty, and a few hours before we fight, we're on duty," said Bad Bear.

"Ah! We no know when we do duty. We told nothing in this army. We never told nothing in Russian Army," laughed Katya. She had already been drinking her share of vodka.

Truck looked around at the Russian officers. Most of them were full of vodka and would be when the attack started. The first shot would help sober them some, but he wondered how many were going to pay for their poor leadership. He reckoned it didn't matter too much, because most of the enlisted men would be in the same shape.

"You do *kazatske*?" asked Katya.

Bad Bear looked at Truck.

"*Kazatske* is the Cossack folk dance. You know, get down on your haunches and kick out a foot at a time," Truck informed him.

"Damn! I'd've been better at this a few years back," Bad Bear said.

Katya led him out in the circle where army officers were dancing. She pushed him into the line of men and stood back to laugh and cheer him on.

Bad Bear held his own for two dances, then he gave up. He joined Katya and stood by her. She hung onto his arm, as much to steady herself as a show of farmilarity.

When Katya learned that Bad Bear was a Native American, she grabbed his hand and pulled him toward the edge of the circle. She said she had seen American movies of American Indians, with war paint, feathers and leathers. A roll in her sleeping bag was in order.

He asked her why that was demanded.

To cement the relations of the Russians and the Americans. Were they not comrades now?

Bad Bear felt he was obliged to add as much cement as possible for the benefit of his country.

The Indian returned to the Americans' area at zero-one-hundred hours. He didn't know about the rest of the United States and Russia, but he knew two people who had been cemented.

17

Truck told his men that the Russians had agreed with most of the existing plan of attack. The plan had been cleaned up some, but there had been no drastic changes. Eagle Attack Team would strike the defenses around the sites where the warheads were located. They would support the attack of the Polish commandos, whose primary mission was to assist the team of Russian nuclear experts to extract the warheads and return them to Russia. The Eagle Attack Team also had the mission of supporting attacks on the rear and main Red Army headquarters. The Russians would attack all known Red Army encampments, keep them pinned down and cover the withdrawal of the Polish commandos and the Eagle Attack Team. The Russians were to provide air cover.

The Eagle Attack Team was to destroy every tank and missile it came in contact with. Intelligence gave the location of new experimental missiles, called SSX-25, as near one of the nuclear warhead storage areas. The Red Army was suspected to have five to ten nuclear warheads.

The team's forward area support group was in place and waiting.

Upon completion of the operation, the team was to form here at this airfield and return to the States.

Were there any questions?

No one spoke up.

Truck was sure that the Russian high command was doing handsprings through their asses because they were to make diversionary attacks and keep the enemy pinned down. Upon completion of the primary mission of the operation, they were to cover the American and Polish withdrawal and remain to clean up the area of operations. He thought it quite fitting.

"Okay, let's get ready to do it," said Truck.

The men broke up to get their equipment ready. Time was getting short.

WO Fullove walked up to Truck and said, "Boss, I've been studying the capabilities of those new computers and systems we put in before we left the States. Them things are awesome. I mean damned awesome!"

Truck considered Fullove to be the best computer expert he had ever met. With him and Okahara working together, the team's helicopters were always serviceable, even under the most dire situations.

"We're sure gonna put 'em through their paces in a few hours," Truck told him.

"I'm sure they're gonna give you everything they got an' then some," Fullove assured him. "An' we got a radar scrambler in them birds now that'll throw off any radar guided missile known to man or devil."

"We don't know what the Red Army is gonna throw at us air-wise, but I bet we'll get both infrared and radar-seeking missiles, along with heat-seekers, tossed our way," said

Truck. He held out his mug as Crackers came by with a coffee pot. This was the last call for coffee before they moved out.

Crackers heard the last part of the conversation. He grinned and told Fullove, "Don't worry, if your computer don't compute, my flying will cover our ass."

"Ah, kiss my ass, ya goddamned swabby," said Fullove. "I gotta get ready to catch that chopper."

The Russians had provided a helicopter for Okahara and Fullove to use to catch up with the forward area team. That gave them time to work on the helicopters up to the last minute. When the team lifted off, the Russian helicopter would fly the two Americans to their destination.

"Retired swabby, my man, *retired*," Crackers called after him. He stood and watched with a grin as Fullove walked off. "Ya know, boss, we got the best two men to work on these birds that ya can find."

"Agreed."

"I just got time to put this pot up. I already got my basketball stored and ready to fly." Crackers went off with the coffee pot.

It'll be soon, Truck said in his mind. He looked at his watch. Five minutes before Zero hour. Truck gave a crooked, wicked smile. Old Red Bear, you're gonna get your ass kicked, then set on fire.

Colonel Hetman Beszczynski looked at Lieutenant Colonel O'Neal and smiled. He said, "We will carry the day over the Russians. I'm sure they wished me and my commandos had stayed in Poland."

"That's okay. They don't think we Americans can cut it either," said O'Neal. "We could eat up their *spetsnaz* boys and they know it."

"Yes, all the world has respect for the American SF,"

admitted Hetman. "No, we, you SF and we Polish commando, must show this Red Army that we can work together and demand respect."

"There's no doubt that we'll earn that respect on this day," said O'Neal.

Willie walked up and told them, "We're ready, we combined Poles and Americans."

"You are somewhat different than most of my other commandos," Hetman told the tall black man with a smile.

"But I bleed red just like your boys, colonel," Willie said, returning the smile.

"Your leader tells me that you also make many others bleed red," said Hetman.

Willie nodded it was so and left to join his assigned group.

"I think it's time for us to perform," O'Neal told Hetman.

They saluted each other and went to join their men.

Dzhaba Groman woke the woman next to him. He was as rutty as an old goat. At sixty-two years of age, he could still perform sexually twice a night, most every night. He was a brutal and demanding lover, having only passion and no *com*passion.

The woman was overweight, smelled of sheep dung and hard soap and had work-worn hands from her peasant surroundings, but she was a woman. He had told her that she could either come to his bed or he would castrate her two sons. He had not informed her that her husband was already a dead man, only that he had been sent away on a job for the Red Army. When she understood that her half-grown sons might be neutered, she went with him to the cabin in the mountains, her face wet with tears, but not arguing with him. She had seen many men such as him in her thirty-six years of life. Dzhaba would search the area later for something better, but at the moment this woman would have to satisfy his needs.

She woke, not realizing where she was for a moment. She knew only that she was in a strange bed and it was not her husband who had a mouth full of breast. She struggled until he bit down hard on the nipple. She gasped in pain.

Dzhaba had pulled open her rough nightgown to expose her breasts. He raised his head and growled, "Do you wish to be screwed by a ram while I watch?"

"Oh, no," she moaned. Oh, God, such a great sacrilege to mankind. The woman had no real conception of how this man had over the years violated every hallowed sacrament of every religion known to man. Defiling women was as easy a task as denying that there was a living God to hold him to account for what he had done here on earth.

"Get up and bend over so I won't have to smell your foul breath," he ordered.

She did as she was told, shuddering with fright as he lifted her nightdress and threw it up over her head.

He suddenly stopped and listened.

She shook even more, wondering if she had displeased him and what her punishment would be. She didn't want to be screwed again by the long piece of hard rubber he had used on her the previous evening. He had used lard to make it penetrate her vagina, but it still had hurt enough to make her scream out. She had finally faked an orgasm to make him quit.

He slapped her on the ass and growled, "I hear helicopters. Many helicopters."

He next heard missiles and machine-gun fire. He was an expert at the game of war. He knew they were being attacked. He left the woman and ran to his clothes. He put them on and yelled at her, "You be here waiting for me when I get back. I don't want you dressed!"

She stood trembling in the cold darkness and nodded her head out of fear, forgetting to answer him out loud.

He gathered his pistol and gear and left the house.

Colonel Georgi Krasnov heard the roar of the helicopters over the groaning engine of his vehicle. He switched off the lights and listened.

Two of his bodyguards jumped out of the military car and stood with their rifles at the ready. The third bodyguard manned the machine gun on a pedestal bolted to the floor in the back compartment of the vehicle.

"Get back in!" ordered Georgi. "We are under attack by some fools."

Georgi's first thought was to get to the nuclear warhead site and get ready to shoot off a missile. He didn't care what the first target was, only that they punish the world for taking everything away from him.

He pushed the button to his radio and called his headquarters. "Attention! Get ready to fire a missile. Call a worldwide alert and inform Warsaw that they are going to receive the first nuclear blast from the Red Army of the People!"

We're going to do it! We're going to attack the world! thought one of the men with Georgi. He knew that he would be with the greatest ruler since Stalin, or he would be dead on this day.

When Pytor heard the helicopters, he ran to headquarters. He hurried inside the building and yelled, "Where is Comrade Georgi?"

The men behind the switchboard stood and said, "The

Colonel is somewhere in the area. He took a car to tour the sites. He felt something was wrong on this night.''

A rocket blast tore into a nearby building, blowing it apart.

"He was right about that," the Don Cossack laughed and started out to do battle. He was happiest when things became unbearable to others.

"Comrade, I am receiving a message from the colonel," the radio man called to him.

Pytor paused to hear the message. A frown crossed his face when he heard Georgi's orders. He looked hard at the radio operator. This man would call the radio team with the long-range transmitter and have them announce to the world that it was now under attack.

"Wait! Do not inform the world. Inform Warsaw first, alone. Then after the first missile is off, we tell the rest of the world," Pytor ordered.

"I must obey my commander!" the man told Pytor in a strained voice. They all knew the brutality of Colonel Krasnov. He would skin any of them alive on a moment's notice. Comrade was just a word to this man.

Pytor's face went mean and he yelled at the man, "Do it now the way I told you! If you vary from my instructions, I will have the pleasure of killing you for disobeying a direct order! Do you understand me?"

"Yes, Comrade. I will obey," the frightened man informed him. He tried to ring the firing location. The line was dead. He keyed his mike and sent a radio message.

When it was finished, Pytor left to find his own battle to fight.

Ivan Ryumin, the transportation expert for the Red Army, jumped from under his blankets with the first blast of missile and cannon fire. The hits were close. God! What is happening? was the first question to cross his mind.

He quickly put on his clothes, the coldness making him shiver uncontrollably. Ivan was not used to this rugged environment he had been placed in. He had always fought the battle of the Communist Party while living in the luxury only members of the Party could afford. Warmth in the cold of winter was one of those luxuries he valued most.

"Come! Come, Nikolai!" he called to his aide as he stood trying to button his shirt. He was having difficulty putting on his clothes.

"Sir, Comrade, what may I do?" Nikolai wanted to know.

"Hold a light for me. I cannot find my boots," complained Ivan.

Nikolai was used to the helpless Ivan. His helplessness was apparent only when it came to the menial things people must do for themselves. At other times he was an overbearing, spoiled little man who garnered respect from others only because they feared his position. Nikolai switched on a flashlight, against his better judgment, and found Ivan's boots under the bed.

Nikolai heard the approaching helicopter and knew at that moment that he should have kept the light off. With a calm he did not feel inside, he told Ivan, "I think this is the end, little comrade."

The light was shining on Ivan's surprised face when the missile crashed through the roof and exploded on the bed. There was no time for goodbyes.

18

The Eagle Attack Team flew in its attack formation of Force Red, Force White and Force Green, with Truck flying control and Donald Day flying observation. They made up Operation Strike Back.

Truck, as Control, call sign "Blue Dad," flew a Blackhawk with his copilot Captain Gene Hunter, U.S. Army, and a crew of two. He was armed with two 7.62mm, electric-driven mini-machine guns, one hanging from each side of the chopper. His helicopter was equipped with the same electronics capability as the Apaches. He could scramble or block radar, see in all low-visual situations, and seek, locate and home in on radio and radar transmissions.

LTC Donald Day, U.S. Air Force, Retired, was Bird Dog, call name "Sky Eye," and flew an O-2 push-and-pull Cessna. A U.S. SF man was assigned on this operation who could speak Russian and Polish and flew with him as spotter. They had the good-guy/bad-guy codes of the Russian Air Force to use as dictated by the tactical situation.

Force Red consisted of two Apaches with Bad Bear Sate-Zalebay, call sign "Red Bear," and WO Edward Horwitz, U.S. Army, in one and Crackers Grahame, call sign "Red Down," and WO Amos Pylant, U.S. Army, in the second one.

Force White consisted of two Apaches with Red Dog Bavaros, call sign "White Dog," and Captain Amos Turki, U.S. Army, in one and WO Roger Miller, U.S. Army, "White Car," and Buddy McGee, U.S. Navy, in the second one.

Force Green consisted of two Apaches with Captain Tyron Riggs, U.S. Army, call sign "Green Dude," and WO Arturo Velasco, U.S. Marine Corps, in one and Wild Bill Flanagan, U.S. Army, call sign "Green Pud," and Tomas Hernandez, U.S. Air Force, in the second one.

Truck looked around his helicopter and could see other aircraft, both fixed-wing and rotory, flying at his altitude. These aircraft carried Polish commandos and Soviet *spetsnaz* troops. He had not seen Russian attack helicopters and jets. He hoped they would stand off until the surprise of the attack by his team achieved its objective and the commandos had time to be inserted.

"Blue Dad. Blue Dad. This is Sky Eye. Received message from friendly ground observation. I read. 'Warheads and SSX-25 missiles remain in location.' Repeat. 'Warheads and SSX-25 missiles remain in location.' Over."

"Sky Eye. I copy. Out," called Truck.

That meant the targets were still in the location reported before. So far, so good. They would hit the Red Army with total surprise.

They had received some good, solid military intelligence about the defensive deployment of the Red Army, but much of its capability was not known. Tactical air was a complete unknown. No one had tested its air capabilities to obtain a definite reading. If the Red Army had a ground force as well as a naval force, it was only reasonable to believe that they had an air force.

"Blue Dad. I am picking up radar signals. They show to originate from a warning system. Over," Horwitz called over the air.

"Operation Strike Back. This is Blue Dad. Switch on anti-radar and locate targets for attack. The first round that pops, we're engaged. Out."

Truck rechecked his instruments and called for an ammunition check by his crew members. He knew it was unnecessary, but prepared warriors win.

The team flew over the outer perimeter and neared the mainline of defense.

"Truck, I spot two men below us with Grail missiles," Hunter reported over the intercom. NATO forces called the SA-7 shoulder-fired missile the "Grail." The Grail was an infrared-seeker.

Truck could see the figures of the two men in his night vision equipment. It looked like the two men were holding SA-7s. Those little missiles could ruin a chopper jockey's day. He dove for the two armed men and their three ammo bearers. He touched off both guns for a short burst. The five men dropped to the ground, dead. As one man with a SA-7 fell, he touched off his missile and it fired, hitting the ground ten feet in front of him.

"I think we got us another shootin' war on our hands, Truck," said Hunter, a happy note in his voice.

Truck continued on course, searching for the area where they believed the nuclear warheads were located. Force Red had the responsibility to neutralize the zone around the nuclear warhead storage area of armor and ground troops. The commandos would then land to secure the area while the special nuclear teams searched for the warheads and took them to safety. Truck wanted to make sure those warheads were out of the area and out of action.

Red Dog called to his wingman, Roger Miller, and said, "Hey, White Car, we're near our targets. Get ready to dance."

"Ah think Ah already hear the fiddler strinkin' up the music," returned Miller.

The mission of Force White was to take out all known ICBM-capable missiles and search for others. Its first targets were the five known SSX-25s.

Riggs called Wild Bill and said, "I think, my man, that our force is near the largest concentration of armor I've ever seen. And, my man, I mean a bunch."

The mission of Force Green was to engage all armor and anti-aircraft weapons it could find. Its primary targets were the armor and air defense weapons around the Red Army's main headquarters. It was also to attack all command structures and communication facilities.

"Then let's get to it. Ah was gettin' bored sittin' at Hood playin' war," Wild Bill called.

"Hell, wild man, you be bored around pussy, ya like war so much," Hernandez told him.

Velasco shot out a few vulgar words in Spanish.

"Ya know, Riggs, Ah can't believe that Truck would put two Mexicans in the same force," said Wild Bill.

"Me neither, my man, but we're stuck with what we got," Riggs informed him.

"Now, black man, ya got the best damned gunner ya've ever flown with," Velasco reminded Riggs.

"You are absolutely right, Spanish-speaking man. You're right as hell," said Riggs.

"Whoa!" cried Wild Bill as he pulled the Apache to the right to dodge an incoming shoulder-fired missile.

"Where is that fucker! I gonna get him in the ass!" called Hernandez.

Wild Bill turned back to search the area. They were flying in dangerous territory now. A hidden man with a shoulder-fired surface-to-air missile could not be found unless he was seen just before he fired or just after. It was the after-he-fired that caused all the trouble.

"There's two of 'em!" called Velasco as he cut loose with the swivel cannon under the chopper's belly. 30mm rounds sprayed the area, kicking up rocks and dirt while mowing down small trees that got in the way. "Take that, pig fuckers!"

"Ya got 'em!" said an excited Wild Bill.

"I love these things! I just love 'em!" called Velasco.

The radio traffic began to get hot and thick.

Eagle Attack Team had their own highly classified radio frequency and their communications were not cluttered by other radio traffic. They had a second radio to communicate with other forces.

"Red Dog! SAM at two o'clock!"

"I got 'em." He gave an unnecessary order to Turki, "Shoot when ready."

A long burst of 30mm cannon fire streamed from beneath the helicopter to reach its target with devastating results. The rockets on the vehicle exploded in bright fireballs.

"Goddamn! There's a Gecko!"

The Gecko was NATO code for the SA-8, a vehicle with six rubber tire wheels, three on each side. It carried four missiles per vehicle and was a radar-seeker.

"Get that fucker!"

"Yeah, don't talk about it."

"Aw, shit!"

"Ah got a Gainful locked in on me!"

"Shake 'em."

"Turn on the goddamned machine." The machine was the anti-radar. The Gainful was the SA-6, a full track with three missiles per vehicle. It was both an infrared and radar-seeker.

"How many SAMs they got anyway?"

"Enough to keep us busy."

Each of the three helicopter forces was engaged in its own battle and not aware or caring about the overall picture.

"Here comes the Ruskies," Truck announced over the intercom. "Damn! They've sent enough of 'em."

Russian attack and transport helicopters filled the air around the mountains.

"I see a bunch of helicopters! There're some old Hips. And there's some little Hazes. And there's the flying tank, the Hind."

"It ain't quite got the stuff as our flying tank."

"No, but it's hell on our armor."

"Not with us around."

The men fired at targets of opportunity when they couldn't spot a target in their assigned mission area.

"What's that? That the new tank killer, the Mi-28?"

"That looks like it. It's called Havoc."

"It looks like it could raise a little of that."

"It still ain't got what our tank killers got."

Nationalistic pride surfaced more around military men than any other segment of society. Most military men reveled in that nationalistic pride and didn't much care about those who were embarrassed about national breast-beating and flag-waving.

Five Russian MiG-17 Fresco-C, basic jet fighters, streaked down past Red Dog. They unloaded their ordnance and flew straight up, getting into position for another run.

"Ya sonsabitches! Get outta my area!" called Red Dog. He switched to the radio used for contacting other forces in the operation. "You ex-Commies in the 17s. Stay outta my area or I'll starting shootin' the sky up!"

"No understand English, American man," came over the air. But the five jets flew off to another area.

"Look at those missiles!" called Buddy.

From his position he could see two SSX-25 missiles that had been moved into position. The SSX-25 was a mobile, three-stage, solid-propellant ICBM. It had a range of about 11,000 kilometers.

"You get the one on the left. I've got the other one," called Red Dog.

"Gotcha."

Both gunners started firing Hellfire missiles at the Russian-built ICBMs. They kept their distance, knowing that a blast from the exploding fuel of the missiles could knock them out of the air.

A MiG-23 swing-wing interceptor with external gun packs under its wings slipped past Miller and Buddy. Buddy saw the Russian MiG, but he didn't pause. He fired another Hellfire. It was a direct hit. The MIG flew close to the missile, poring cannon fire into the missile launch area. The blast from the SSX-25 slapped the jet fighter sideways from its course and it flew into the mountainside.

"Rack up one more dummy in this cruel cold world!" Buddy cried out.

"Damn thing's got a blast, don't it?"

The second ICBM went up in a small mushroom cloud of smoke and fire when it was hit by a Hellfire.

"Where's those other dudes?" asked Red Dog, more to himself than to the other three.

"We gotta circle the area and hunt 'em out," was Miller's suggestion.

''Let's do it. And stay close. Those damned Russians are buzzing around the area like a bunch of dodo birds.''

''They sure gonna get themselves wiped out like that.''

The two Apaches banked and started a systematic search of the area for the other three Russian missiles.

19

Vladimir Bokey stopped the vehicle and watched the helicopters attack positions in different areas of the mountains. It seemed that each attack was made on his most important installations and defense positions. The attackers had good military intelligence.

I have a mole, was the first thing that entered his head.

He knew what he was going to do. There was one warhead located in an area he could get to from his present location. It was his fail-safe missile. He would move the warhead to the location of an old SS-11 he had managed to have transported to the mountains and dug in. It was not a new generation missile, but it had been tested over time and found to be reliable.

He pushed the button on his handset and called his forward headquarters. He asked to speak to Colonel Krasnov.

"He is not here, sir," the man called into his mike.

Vladimir could hear explosions and machine-gun fire in

the background. The headquarters was under a full-scale attack. Vladimir said, "If you can reach Colonel Krasnov, inform him that I am going to Site 203. I repeat, I am going to 203. Get that message to him."

He threw the headset up against the dash of the vehicle. I will lose it all! Who *are* these people?

As he sat, two black helicopters with no markings passed overhead. They had not seen the vehicle. If he had had the engine running or had been transmitting over the radio, they would have picked the vehicle up with their instruments.

After the helicopters cleared the area, Vladimir took a chance and called the man in charge of the single warhead he wanted. He told him, "Take the vehicle and move to Site 203. And be careful. There are very sophisticated helicopters in the air with the ability to track vehicles by their ignition, heat, radar and radio transmissions. You have direct orders to fire the missile whether I am present at the location or not. Do you understand?"

The man told Vladimir that he understood the order.

Vladimir knew that the helicopters he had seen had been built by Americans. He was sure they were AH-64 Apache helicopters. Since they had no markings, they must be assigned to a highly classified unit. It would be a unit that had every type of new equipment the Americans could develop. He, and others in the Soviet government, had wished for some of that equipment themselves. But it would take a number of years before they could steal enough information from American projects to develop their own equipment.

He told his men, "We'll go to our next destination very slowly. Keep checking for approaching helicopters. If you fail to be on the lookout and let one approach us without detecting it, I will guarantee you a funeral before nightfall."

He started the vehicle and drove a hundred yards. He stopped again and switched off the engine. He didn't dare use his radio any longer. Was he being too careful? Was he paranoid?

He didn't know the answer to either question. He only knew that he was not going to challenge those huge flying monsters overhead.

Willie peered over the shoulder of the pilot of the Mi-17, or "Hip-H" as NATO called the Russian-built helicopter. The Mi-17 was normally used as a cargo carrier, but it also had the ability to carry troops. There were fold-down web seats, but Willie spent most of his time on his feet, his head rubbing against the top of the aircraft. This Hip-H also had weapons pods hanging from winglets on both sides.

Lieutenant Colonel Klemens Takarzewski, the executive officer of the Polish commando regiment, stood beside Willie. As in the SF, Rangers and Delta Force of the American military, these Polish commanders went with their troops.

Four other Mi-17s flew in formation with the lead helicopter. Mi-24s, known as the Hind in the West, tank-killer gunship helicopters, flew cover.

When Willie saw a flight of Russia's new tank killing Mi-28s, called the Havoc by the West, he growled in anger. The idea that someone stole or sold AH-64 plans to the Soviets ran through his mind.

The Havoc had the uncanny look of an Apache. Each Havoc had a swivel 23mm cannon under its chin and 16 AT-6 Spiral missiles hanging from its two winglets.

The ground forces defending the Red Army rear head-quarters began firing at the approaching aircraft. Russian Hinds went into action, spraying down the area with cannon fire and blasting away at tanks with their anti-tank missiles.

A 7.62mm round from an AK-47 fired by a soldier on the ground went through the floor of the helicopter at Willie's feet and burst through the ceiling near his head. It missed the rotor blades whirling overhead.

"Damn!" exclaimed Willie. "Feels like I'm back in combat."

Klemens looked over at Willie and smiled. "I think it will get dangerous soon."

The Polish officer knew that the American had much more experience in combat than he had. But neither he nor his men would shirk from gunfire once the battle was joined.

An SA-7 round hit the rear strut of a commando loaded Mi-17 to their right. The helicopter shuddered and slowly spiraled to the ground as the pilot fought to control the aircraft. They did not see it hit the ground.

Willie was glad another wave of five helicopters was close behind this one. He may have had to make the attack all by himself if the rest of the men hadn't come in.

The helicopter set down and the commandos jumped out. Willie jumped out into the wash of the rotor blades as the aircraft was on its way back up. These guys had really been training. Melting snow and thin ice thrown up by the air turbulence stung his face.

A spray of machine-gun fire pinned the men down.

Willie made a quick assessment of the situation, stood up and blasted away with his M-16; he charged the point of least resistance. Never get pinned down at no time, ran through Willie's mind. If ya do, you're dead.

A commando lieutenant yelled for his men to follow the tall American. They jumped up as one, firing to the left and right of Willie to kill or pin down the enemy with full automatic fire.

Willie fired into a foxhole as he jumped in feet first on top of two Red Army soldiers. He didn't have to use his bayonet. Both were dead from the rapid fire of his rifle.

Two Polish commandos jumped into the hole with him. They grinned. Willie returned their grins as one warrior to another.

Willie looked around. He saw a small building to one side of the main headquarters building. He figured it was quarters for one of the leaders. The second wave of commandos had come in and the other buildings were being attacked. He stood up and motioned for the two men to follow him. They followed without hesitation.

As he ran around the cabin, Willie noticed that it had been hit by a missile and most of the back wall was blown away. He could see that it had hit a storage room, went through it and took away most of the inner wall of the main room.

He stopped near the front door. The two commandos flanked the other side of the door. He nodded his head that he was ready, and one of the commandos kicked open the door. Willie jumped into the room and stepped to one side, his back against the wall. The two commandos followed him into the room, ready to fire at any sign of resistance.

The missile had blasted a hole in the wall just above the bed. The mangled body of a woman lay half in and half out of the bed. The front of her nightgown had been torn away. A man lay on the floor, his pants down around his ankles. Most of his head and his right shoulder were missing. Dzhaba, the raper of women and little girls, had returned for one last fling.

"I can't tell if this guy died with a smile on his face or not," Willie said in English. "He ain't got no face left."

He saw a stack of papers and a briefcase on a small table in the corner of the room. He was an expert and did his job as such. He gathered up all papers he could find and placed what he could in the case. The rest he placed in a cotton flour sack he found on a counter. He took them with him as he left the building to search of other targets.

* * *

The Red Army lieutenant in charge of the warhead Vladimir had directed to move to Site 203 ordered the vehicle moved out of the cave. When it was clear, he directed the move to the location of the SS-11. He and his men would accomplish their orders, even though he was now out of contact with any leader. He knew that Warsaw was to be his target no matter what happened. The lieutenant knew that Vladimir hated the Poles and blamed them for the fall of the Soviets. He always claimed that it was that rabble-rousing union leader in Gdansk that led to the eventual collapse of the Red Party. If that Pole had been killed on the spot, none of this would have happened.

The truck pulled up beside the silo that had been constructed for the missile. The lieutenant directed the truck with the small crane to lift off the high explosive warhead and place the nuclear warhead in its place. If one of those devil imperialist air weapons didn't locate them, they would shoot off the first nuclear weapon in anger since World War II.

Georgi Krasnov thought it was probably a lost cause from the moment the Russian army showed up. When he saw the American-built AH-64 Apache helicopters, what doubt he had turned to certainty. But he was a professional soldier. He would not let himself fall to the hated Russian leaders who had given up the course set by Lenin and nurtured by Stalin. He would die first, either by the bullet of the enemy or by his own hand.

He jumped out of the vehicle as soon as the helicopters had come on scene. He knew the capabilities of these flying monsters. They were years ahead of the Mi-28 that the Soviets had recently deployed. These helicopters obviously had every known new weapon and detection system in the inventory of the United States military.

A vehicle eased around a trail and out of sight. He got a look at it through his night-sighting device before it disappeared around the bend. Vladimir was on his way to a mission. It could only be to cast a nuclear warhead at the capitol of Poland. That man hated the opposition in the Soviet Union as much as that crazy Don Cossack, Georgi growled in his mind. Let him go do his thing. He was going to make a stand with his beautiful missiles, the SSX-25s.

A helicopter came at them from the left. One of his men stopped to open up with his AK-47. Georgi kept moving. The fool. If that helicopter can kill the largest tank in existence, what protection would a mere man have out in the open?

A burst from the 30mm cannon on the Apache cut loose, spraying the area. Tree limbs fell to the ground, and pieces of wood splinters and metal from the cannon rounds whizzed through the air.

Georgi hugged mother earth in an infantryman's embrace and cursed the peasant minds of his men. He lay a moment longer and the aircraft flew on out of sight. The instruments of the Apache had searched out and killed every man who had not hidden his body from the heat-seeking instruments.

"There is no hope," muttered Georgi. "But I will die fighting for the Motherland and the Red Party!"

He jumped to his feet, determined to reach the site of the SSX-25s. There he would arm and fire every damned missile. He also had SS-20 IRBM missiles he could use for three of the warheads. He could hit Warsaw with the first missile, even if Vladimir also hit it with a separate launch. Then Prague was next, followed by Berlin, Paris, London and maybe Moscow itself. The government in Moscow had sold out the Motherland and had gone to bed with the imperialists of the West. It deserved no protection from him and his men.

Vladimir has at least one warhead. That means I will have two more after my initial attacks. One should be for Peking, the capitol of the Chinese and the followers of the heretic, Mao Tse-tung. He sucked in his breath at the final thought. One will be for the most hated enemy of all, Washington, D.C., capitol of the most vile of all capitalist pigs.

He ran on, dogging trees and shrubs, with a curled smile of hatred on his drawn lips.

20

Jets started screaming in, guns, rockets and missiles blazing. They wore Red Stars on their sides and wings, the markings of the Red Army. They were the enemy. Other jets appeared with Russian markings and filled the air. Dogfights between the once-united people broke out.

A missile zoomed in front of Truck's helicopter.

"Damn!" breathed Hunter out loud.

"Glad these new instruments are working," replied a calm Truck.

"Ain't that a goddamned fact!"

Truck spun the Blackhawk around to face the oncoming Soviet Hind. He and Hunter would have been thrown out the doors and left behind in midair if they had not been wearing seatbelts.

The Hind-D sprayed the Blackhawk with its 12.7mm gun. A few rounds hit the rotor blades. The tough blades swatted the bullets away like they were pesky mosquitoes.

"I got that sucker!" shouted Hunter. Then he cut loose with more bursts from the electric Gatlin guns.

The Hind slipped off to run for cover. It was a mistake and exposed his tender rear quarters where there were no armor plates. The 7.62mm guns of the Americans hit the blades and an engine on the port side. The Hind's engine caught fire, and large chunks began to fly off the damaged blades. The Hind banked over on its side and shook as it plummeted to the ground. It crashed with an explosion that scattered twisted metal and crewmen over the mountainside.

"I'm glad that thing wasn't an E-model with Spirals," said Truck. The Spiral was a Soviet anti-tank missile that could also be used for other purposes in an emergency, like shooting down another helicopter at close range.

"Mark up one more kill for old Truck and Hunter," the captain said. "We'll put our crews' names right under the Red Star."

"Yeah, I can dig that," one of the men called over the intercom.

"We'd better look up," said Truck. "Here comes a damned jet our way."

"Dispense that chaff and cut on the wiggle machine!" cried Hunter as he flipped switches that would help divert radar or infrared seeking missiles.

Truck faced the jet and opened up with both guns, squeezing the trigger in a long burst. His guns could not destroy a Hind-E face to face, but the 7.62mm rounds could and did shoot down jets.

The jet pilot pulled back on his stick and banked to the right for a roll away from the oncoming helicopter. This maneuver exposed his tender belly, and two bullets passed through the bottom of the aircraft and hit the pilot's legs. The wings of the jet were stitched with bullets, and tracer rounds set the fuel on fire. The jet exploded and the pieces fell to the ground.

"Ain't we bad asses?" asked Hunter.

The rest of the crew agreed.

Bad Bear saw the two jets on the screen at the same time Horwitz saw them. They were Yakovlev, or Yak, jets.

"Those guys are the baddies," Horwitz said over the intercom.

"They'd better be 'cause they're dead," growled Bad Bear. Then he called over the air, "Blue Dad. This is Red Bear. There are two Yaks coming down on you. I will engage."

The two Yak-28P, two-seat, all-weather fighters carrying two Anab air-to-air missiles each, dove down from out of the clouds toward Truck's Blackhawk. Their night vision systems were not as good as those of the Americans, but they had no trouble spotting the slower moving Blackhawk.

"I gotcha, boys," Bad Bear announced. "Do it, Horwitz."

Horwitz squeezed the trigger, sending off first one of the Arrows and then the second one. He announced, "On the way."

The American air-to-air missiles sped to their targets. Both missiles had overriding systems that let them push through any known anti-radar or anti-infrared system.

The first missile hit its target with a blast of smoke and fire. A wing fell off the Yak and it cartwheeled into the ground. The second Yak tried to evade the oncoming flash of death, but he could not outmaneuver the swift Arrow. The missile flew up its exhaust vent as the Yak tried to retreat to safer airspace. It exploded from within and the force of the blast sent pieces flying through the air.

"I blind-sided ya, assholes," growled Bad Bear.

"Thanks heaps," breathed Hunter in appreciation.

"We aim to please and keep our good buddies alive," returned Bad Bear.

Bad Bear and Horwitz rejoined Crackers and Pylant and flew off to other adventures.

Force Green began its systematic attack on the antiaircraft systems of the Red Army. Every time a ground-to-air missile showed up on radar, it was dead meat. With their communications systems destroyed or badly damaged, the Red Army leaders didn't have the means to inform their troops that the attacking American helicopters had sophisticated devices to pick up radar, infrared and radio signals.

The American helicopters flew low to the ground and were masked much of the time by ridges and mountaintops. The SAMs could not use their radars for long-range shooting. But that still didn't make life easy for the Apaches.

The anti-radar system on Riggs's Apache emitted a fast beat, indicating that the SAM radar had detected them. Velasco called, "We've got a SA-8 locked in on us!"

Riggs glanced at the screen and turned the Apache toward the SAM.

"No, man, ya got three of them things on your butts!" said Hernandez.

"Well, hell, man, do something!" yelled Velasco as he sighted in on the missile launcher. A burst from his Chain Gun went straight and true. The 30mm rounds knocked tires off the vehicle and a missile exploded, finishing the job.

Hernandez sprayed down one Gecko and Wild Bill rose higher to get a good shot at the third dug-in SAM. Hernandez called, "Missile coming our way!"

"Heave to!" yelled Wild Bill as he pulled hard to the right and dropped down lower to the ground. When he was sure he had evaded the missile, he shot back up for a look at the Gecko.

Hernandez sighted in with his infrared guidance system and touched off a Hellfire. "Take that, ya mothers!"

"Hey! Hey man, look at that tank, will ya?" asked Velasco.

Riggs looked at the screen. "What ya got?"

"I think it's that T-80 light tank them Reds was building," Velasco told him.

"Then get him," Riggs told him.

"Yeah, my babies can knock out anything you guys can build," said Velasco. A Hellfire blasted off from its rack and flew to the tank. The tank was slapped sideways by the impact, and when the missile exploded, it set off the ammunition inside the tank and blew the turret off. Velasco gave a wicked laugh, and said to his Hellfire, "Thanks, baby."

Most of the T-80 and T-72 tanks were dug in with their main guns pointed skyward so they could be used in an antiaircraft mode. The tanks cut loose on the two Apaches. They fired every gun they had, including their main guns. The T-72 had a 125mm main gun and the T-80 carried a 76.2mm gun. Their main guns weren't accurate when firing in this manner, but once on the way the rounds could not be deterred by any system the Apaches had on board. Fortunately the cannon round was propelled only by the force of gunpowder and had no guidance system.

The Apaches didn't worry about the 12.7mm rounds coming their way. The hard bodies and toughened rotor blades of their aircraft could withstand rounds up to 23mm without any problem. Many enemy gunners were dismayed when they saw their large machine-gun rounds bounce off the body of an Apache or ricochet off the whirling rotor blades.

The team used up its ammunition and flew off to the

forward area team for a quick refuel and rearm. Within a short time, they were back over the battlefield, blasting away at the enemy armor and SAMs.

"Man, ain't we hot shits!" laughed Hernandez.

A missile flew past the body of the Apache and hit the tip of a rotor blade. The helicopter lurched to one side and then bounced back in the direction it was going. Wild Bill hung on to the controls, trying to keep the aircraft at a level attitude. The out-of-balance blades shook the aircraft and rattled the men's teeth.

"It's gonna shake itself to pieces!" called Wild Bill. "Grab those damned controls and help me hang on to this thing!"

Wild Bill kept the ground situation in mind as he turned the helicopter away from the enemy defense positions and looked for a cleared area suitable for an emergency landing. A large piece flew from the damaged blade and smacked into another blade, shearing off another chunk. The helicopter shook violently and started down toward the ground, gaining speed as it went.

"Hold on, Hernandez! We're gonna have one hell of a landing!" called Wild Bill.

Man, ain't that a fact, Hernandez thought as he hung on to the controls.

It was dark, and they had a hard time judging the distance to the ground. Wild Bill made a quick judgment and reversed pitch to gyro into the ground. The Apache did its best to flare out and make a soft landing, but there was too much damage to the blades.

The helicopter hit the ground with a crash and bounced once before settling down. The force of the impact broke the front bubble loose, and it flew off into the night, exposing Hernandez to a piece of flying rotor blade. It hit his right arm just below the shoulder, nearly severing it.

Both men sat in their seats, stunned from the impact, but still alive. The Apache had been called the most "crash-worthy" helicopter ever built. It had a rollbar configuration built around the two cockpits, and the seats were designed to survive the impact of a crash landing. It proved itself on this night.

"Are you all right?" Wild Bill asked over the air.

Hernandez groaned. He was barely semiconscious from the shock of the blade hitting him, and his head was down on his chest.

Wild Bill threw back the canopy and climbed to where Hernandez sat strapped in his seat. He pulled off the man's helmet and felt his jugular vein for a pulse. He found one.

"Green Pud! Give me a report! Give me a report!" Riggs radioed.

"We're alive. Hernandez has a bad wound. I'm taking him out of the chopper now," returned Wild Bill. His own hip was screaming from the pain of a break. "When I disconnect, I'll go to my emergency portable radio."

"I copy that. We'll fly cover," Riggs told him.

As he was talking, Velasco opened up with his 30mm gun on a squad of men making its way toward the downed Apache.

"Stand by. We'll be there in seconds to pick up the downed men," Truck called to Riggs.

"I'll keep the enemy off. But you'd better hurry before they send out a larger force."

Two Soviet PT-76 amphibious light tanks rolled up over a hill and out onto a trail. They started shooting at the downed helicopter with their 76.2mm main guns and machine guns. The rounds knocked down trees before they reached the helicopter.

"Get 'em!" yelled Riggs.

"I got 'em in my sights," Velasco told him. The TADS

system calculated the information the Hellfires needed to hit their targets, and Velasco pressed the buttons when they were ready. Two Hellfires blasted out, one going to a close target and the other seeking out an objective to the rear.

Two explosions sounded and it was "scratch two tanks."

"I see a clearing. I'm going to fire a burst into it. Can you reach it?" asked Truck, pressing the trigger of his starboard gun.

"Yeah. I see where to go. We're on the way," said Wild Bill.

"Riggs, blow that thing once we clear the area," ordered Truck.

"Roger that, boss."

Wild Bill slung Hernandez over his shoulder and limped off to the LZ Truck had pointed out. He was hurting badly before he reached the pickup spot, but he wasn't about to quit. He had heard some bad tails about what happened to Russian prisoners.

Truck lowered the Blackhawk into the small clearing. He set the front wheels down on the side of the mountain, keeping the rear wheel up off the ground because of the steepness of the terrain.

One of the crewmen jumped out of the Blackhawk and ran to meet Wild Bill and take his load from him. They ran to the helicopter as fast as Wild Bill's broken hip would allow and got aboard.

Truck added pitch to the blades and the Blackhawk shot straight up out of the LZ, quickly clearing the tree tops. "I'm heading for the forward area team. I will return," he said over the command net. "Green Pud, join Force White."

"That's an afirmative, boss," said Riggs and turned his helicopter to search out Red Dog and Roger Miller.

Truck swung the helicopter toward the north and flew to

the forward area team. There he dropped the two injured men off, refueled and rearmed and returned to the battle.

In the meantime, Velasco aimed at the body of the downed Apache and let fly with a Hellfire. The blast of the anti-tank missle scattered pieces of the helicopter over the mountainside. Velasco finished cleaning up with the 30mm gun, shredding what remained of the Apache.

"Damn, it's a sad thing to shoot hell out of an Apache!" exclaimed Riggs.

"Ain't it a fact," agreed Velasco.

After their job was finished, they flew off to join Red Dog's force.

21

Bad Bear and Crackers swung up and down the valley where the SSX-25s were located, taking out missiles, armor and SAM sites as they went. Horwitz and Pylant were deadly accurate with all the weapons systems on their aircraft. The enemy didn't have a chance.

"The LZ is clear," announced Bad Bear to Stu, who was with the Polish commandos.

"Message received," Stu replied. He informed Hetman that they had been given the all-clear to land and search out the warheads. The Apaches would continue to fly cover and take out any would-be attackers coming their way.

The commandos landed and unloaded from their helicopters.

The Russian nuclear specialists landed in the huge Soviet-built Mi-26s, called "Halos" in the West, heavy-lift helicopters. The Mi-26 had the same load-carrying capability as an American C-130.

Small four-wheeled trucks with cranes drove out of the

rear of the Mi-26s. These vehicles would be used to lift and carry the nuclear warheads back to the large helicopters for transport back to Russia.

The three areas used by the Red Army to store the warheads had been located. Stu went along with the Polish commandos to secure those areas while the Russians got their gear together to pick up the warheads. A security team of commandos was left with the two Mi-26s.

Four more Mi-26 helicopters suddenly appeared in the sky. They had the markings of the Russian Air Force. They landed near the other two Mi-26s and unloaded a company of Russian paratroopers.

The paratroop commander went to Hetman and Stu and explained that they would guard the Mi-26s. That would relieve the commandos from that duty so they could rejoin their unit.

With their full complement of troops, the commandos went out in three groups to secure the warhead sites.

Halo and Hind helicopters started landing in strategic spots and proceeded to unload troops. Intensive firefights broke out, the Russians pressing hard against the Red Army. The fight was hard, and unrelenting pressure was brought against the Red defensive positions.

The plan to drive wedges between the troops securing the warheads and the enemy began to work. In a short time, the area was cleared of all Red Army defenders, and the commandos put up defensive perimeters around the storage areas to protect them against a Red counterattack. The caves were open, and the small trucks with cranes started retrieving the warheads and taking them under guard to the helicopters.

Truck watched the vehicles below him carrying the

warheads. They looked like ants foraging for food, and after finding it, carrying it back to their nests.

"Blue Dad. Blue Dad. This is Blue Toy. We have found only eight warheads. I repeat. We have found only eight warheads. Over." Stu stood next to Hetman as he called Truck.

"Blue Toy. Retrieve those eight and get out of the area. You have accomplished your mission. Out," called Truck. He watched the commandos retreat to their assigned helicopters.

Where was that other warhead? Or were there only eight to begin with? Or are there more? thought Truck. They would have to leave the search for the missing warhead to the Russians.

Red Dog and Roger Miller flew in search of other missiles. Their team had taken out every missile it could find around the SSX-25 sites, plus all armor and antiaircraft weapons. They wanted to destroy as many missiles as they could find. A missile with a standard high explosive warhead fired at some capitol city could cause a psychological trauma with worldwide repercussions.

Riggs pulled his Apache up in line with Red Dog and Miller. Miller gave a thumbs-up to Riggs and Velasco.

"White Dog! White Dog! This is Green Dude. We are joining your force as ordered and are on station. Over." called Riggs.

"Welcome and sorry about Wild Bill and Hernandez. But this is war and I aim to fight it," said Red Dog. The old air force lieutenant colonel was having the time of his life.

"Bear, I got a nuclear warning on my instruments," Horwitz told Bad Bear.

"You've homed in on it?"

"Yep. Got that sucker. It's not more than two klicks away and sittin' still. That means it's on the nose of a missile," warned Horwitz.

"Damn!" said Bad Bear. He pointed the Apache in the direction Horwitz called out.

"Lead on! We're with you!" called Crackers.

"That goddamn thing's armed, Bear!"

"What the hell ya want me to do?"

Bear put the nose down and opened the throttle. The bird flew full out, the powerful piece of machinery giving its all.

"I got it directly below us, but I can't see it," Horwitz told Bear.

"Damn! It must be in a hole."

"I'll search for a silo."

Red Army missile experts had taken the shield off the warhead and armed it. Calculations were being made for it to hit Warsaw dead center. Either World War III would start or they would hold the world hostage.

"I got it! I got it!" cried Horwitz. "To the left, ten degrees. There it is!"

"I see it. Where's the control for this bastard?"

After a short search, Horwitz told him, "Twenty meters right and up fifty meters. See that small sandbagged building?"

"Blast hell outta the thing before they punch the thing out."

Horwitz read the instruments and waited to punch out the Hellfire. It was done in a split second.

The Red Army team was busy getting the missile ready to fire. A guard looked up and saw the two Apaches against the dark sky. He raised his rifle and sent off a burst, yelling an alert at the top of his voice. The burst of fire was an effective warning in and of itself.

The Red Army lieutenant held to his post, ready to fire

the missile as soon as his instruments gave a proper readout. He was safe from most weapons in the heavily sandbagged building he was in. The poor guy didn't figure on an Apache and a Hellfire missile system that cut through sandbags like butter.

The Hellfire hit the sandbag wall dead center. The force of the missile penetrated the sandbags and forced the warhead into the small building before it went off. Horwitz had punched out one of the two missiles he had with delayed fuses. The blast tore the men inside to pieces and mingled body parts with equipment parts. None of them worked after the mix.

"Blue Dog! Blue Dog! Have located an armed warhead sittin' on top of an SS-11," called Bad Bear. "It is armed and ready to fire."

"Lead us to it," called Stu.

Horwitz switched on a homing device to bring Stu to the proper location.

A missile passed by the port side of Crackers's Apache. "Where'd that damned thing come from?"

"I've got 'em! I've got 'em!" called Pylant.

Their mission was to keep all armor and antiaircraft out of action while Bad Bear and Horwitz took out all defenses around the missile.

Three tanks dug in with their guns pointing skyward in an antiaircraft mode fired their main guns and machine guns at the Apache. A 76.2mm round from a T-76 hit the helicopter in the right front side and nearly spun it out of control. The round was a dud and didn't go off, but the impact left a gaping hole in the Apache and put the 30mm cannon out of action.

Crackers was slammed to one side of the cockpit when the round hit. He fought to regain control of the helicopter. It dove down close to the ground before he brought it back up to proper elevation and to a proper attitude. He yelled, "Instrument check!"

After a quick check, Pylant returned with, "A-okay!"

"Then find a goddamned tank, any tank, and kill that fucker!" screamed Crackers. He compensated for the drag and pull from the hole in the nose of the Apache and kept flying.

The two Americans put all of their experience together to search out and destroy tank after tank. They found ground-to-air missiles in their search and took them out as they went. When they ran out of ammunition, Crackers called to Bad Bear, "We gotta go rearm, Bear!"

"Go! We'll be with you shortly," replied Bad Bear.

Crackers pointed his helicopter north and opened the throttles on the two General Electric engines. Wind blew through the gaping hole in the helicopter, setting up a loud howl. It took all of Crackers's flying experience, but the retired navy aviator held his course and subdued the lurching machine.

Crackers called to the forward area team, "Have hole blown in chopper. Need doctoring when I get there. Get ready for major cosmetic operation."

"We're here and ready," the forward base radioed back.

They flew through hostile airspace unarmed. They had expended their last two Arrows on a MiG and a Havoc, and their cannon was inoperative.

Vladimir saw the two Apaches attacking the area where the SS-11 with the nuclear warhead was located. He stopped running and watched; anger made his face turn red. All he could do was stand there and watch his dream go up in smoke and fire.

The Apaches finished their attack, and one left the scene and turned to the north. The second one started scouting the area. One of Vladimir's men fired in anger at the American helicopter with his AK-47.

Horwitz read off instruments and located the AK-47. He touched of a burst of 30mm cannon fire and growled, "Even you ain't gonna get by with that, little boy."

Vladimir did not have time to rebuke his man before he himself was torn to pieces by 30mm rounds. He and his men died, their dreams unfulfilled.

Willie watched the Russian Army troops swarm over the area, chopping up Red Army soldiers as they went. It didn't matter whether the men were dead or not, only that there was a body to attack. Willie wondered if all men were as brutal to their fellow countrymen when they warred against each other. He shook his head in remembrance. He already knew the answer. He had spent years in Laos and Vietnam while those two countries butchered themselves.

Klemens walked over to where Willie stood. The sun was coming up, and they had been fighting for over four hours. He smiled, "I think we show Russians we good warriors."

"I think you showed this American," said Willie with a grin.

"If you come to Poland someday, we have a good time."

"I might just do that," Willie told him.

A Russian colonel walked up to them. Klemens saluted. The colonel looked closely at Willie and then told Klemens in Russian, "You can take your soldiers and go. Get out of my area."

Klemens looked at him a moment and turned to order his radio man to call in their units.

Willie didn't understand the words, but he knew the Russian was not a friendly individual. "What'd this guy say?"

"He said for us to get out of his area," Klemens said.

Willie looked at the Russian and then to Klemens. "If he don't understand English, will you tell him something for me? I mean, *tell* him—and don't be diplomatic about it?"

"What?"

"Tell that sack of shit I have an old American saying for him."

Klemens spoke to the Russian. They all stood waiting. Klemens said, "I wait your words."

"Tell him to go fuck himself and the horse he rode in on."

Klemens paused for a moment, and then a grin spread across his mouth and his eyes brightened. He told the Russian what the American had said.

Surprise crossed the Russian officer's face, then he looked at Willie in anger.

Willie turned his back on him and walked off laughing. Klemens followed.

Crackers and Pylant climbed out of the Apache and looked at the gaping hole in their bird. Pylant gulped and shook his head.

WO Jackson Okahara walked up to the Apache and looked at the hole. He told Crackers and Pylant, "It'll take a while. Go get coffee."

Fullove walked up to them and said, "Ya may not get back into the fight."

"Don't tell me that—just get us airborne," spat Crackers.

"We'll do a helluvalot better if you two get out of here," Okahara informed them, turning to the problem at hand.

Crackers and Pylant walked to the truck that had the coffeepot.

Daglarie and Selma picked out the route most likely to be used by retreating Red Army forces. They set up ambushes so they could block any retreating enemy and support each other.

And retreating Reds came pouring down from the mountains. The two Americans and their Azerbaidzhan allies caught the Reds by surprise and cut them down, one group after another. It was surprising that one group after another ran into the slaughter area even though there were bodies lying all over the area, yet they never slowed down.

A group of Reds heard firing up ahead. The leader was an old professional sergeant with many years' experience in Soviet wars. He sent his two scouts, former Soviet *spetnaz* troopers, ahead to reconnoiter the area.

The two soldiers returned to inform the sergeant of the situation. The sergeant nodded and made a plan to work around to the rear of the ambushing forces. When in place, he would attack.

Selma heard one of his men cry out in surprise and pain. He turned in time to see the man cut down by a man in a Soviet uniform swinging an entrenching tool. The sharpened edge of the shovel took most of the top of the Azerbaidzhan's head off.

The American jumped to his feet and started firing at the two shovel-bearing Reds. The two men also carried PPS submachine guns, firing as they moved toward the Azerbaidzhan force. Two rounds hit Selma, one in the right arm and the second high in his left shoulder.

Selma stood. Both of his arms dropped to his side from the paralyzing shock of his wounds. He yelled, "Come on, ya cocksuckers! Come and get me!"

Two men jumped to his side and started firing their AK-47s. They laid down a field of withering fire while Ata grabbed the American and pulled him to the ground.

The attack from the rear by the Reds didn't affect the soldierly conduct of the Azerbaidzhans. They made a stand and stopped the attack cold. Then they ran out into their killing zone and cleaned up by making sure every attacker was dead.

Selma radioed Daglarie and told him, "I'm hit, big guy. I'm hit."

"How bad?" asked Daglarie.

"Arm and shoulder. I can hang on for a while, but I'm gonna need medical attention soon," Selma replied.

"I'll call for a pickup," said Daglarie. He called the SF battalion commander for a medical pickup.

An SF medical expert flew in to pick up Selma. He came in on a Russian helicopter from the combat area at the foot of the mountains and returned with Selma to the Eagle Attack Team's forward base. All wounded and killed Americans were transported to the forward area team and then shipped to the rear.

Daglarie and his forces continued to hold the area. Other men on horseback patrolled nearby and stopped retreating Reds who tried to run out onto the steppe. The fleeing Red Army soldiers didn't want to bother the indigenous people of Azerbaidzhan. All they hoped for was to flee the attacking helicopters and soldiers who had destroyed their dreams of a world dominated by Communism. They would do their best to work their way back home and keep their involvement with the Red Army a secret from everyone.

The battle was confusing, as are all situations where men come together to kill each other. Few, and none doing the fighting, know the status of a battle or its results until it's finished. It was no different in the mountains of Azerbaidzhan that day. The Americans were told they and the Poles and the Russians had won. That being so, they were ready to return to their aircraft and leave the mopping up to the Russians. The longer they hung around, the more likely they would have outsiders climbing all over themselves and their Apaches. This they could not allow.

"Let's return to our transportation back home, boys," called Truck.

A "roger" was given by the surviving Apaches. The battle was over and had been won. The mop up, capture and disposition of the Red Army leaders and soldiers would be left to the Russian Army. That was of no concern to the Eagle Attack Team. They were warriors, not peacemakers.

22

Red Dog led Roger Miller and Riggs through a low saddle in the mountains. The three Apaches had made five trips back to the forward base to reload and refuel. They reloaded with 16 Hellfire anti-tank missiles, 4 Arrow air-to-air missiles and 1,200 30mm cannon rounds each time. That was a lot of firepower and its delivery turned many tanks, armored vehicles and enemy missles into scrap metal.

"Look at that line of tanks and SAMs!" exclaimed Amos Turki.

"Let's get 'em," said Red Dog.

"Hey, Dog, ya think we can handle that many?" asked Miller.

"We can give it a try," was Red Dog's answer. He dropped the nose down and pointed it toward the defensive line of armor and air-defense weapons.

"I gonna do it. I follow you anywhere, my man," called Riggs.

"This looks like a final defense position," said Turki.

"Then we'll make it their final defense," Red Dog told him.

A fusillade of tank cannon fire and machine-gun rounds flew toward the three Apaches. Turki was an old hand at riding in the front seat and having small arms hit the windshield of the cockpit and bounce off harmlessly. But he was now facing tank cannon rounds, and one of those things could knock him completely out of his cockpit. A cannon round flew under the power it received from a blast of powder, and its guidance system was an aimed shot from the long barrel of the tank. There were no systems that could deter its course. He bared his teeth, sang an Arab war song and read off targets and punched the proper buttons. He fired Hellfires at hard targets and cannon rounds at SAMs. He soon forgot the free-flying cannon fire from the tanks and got down to enjoying his job.

Miller swallowed hard a couple of times and followed the old air force colonel. He broke off to the left of the lead Apache to give Buddy a clear shot at the enemy below.

"Sweet Mother of Jesus," breathed Buddy, looking at the screen in front of him. He was glad it was night so he could only see their images on the instruments and not the real thing. After a few fiery tracers flew past his cockpit, he began to feel like most warriors—"it ain't my time to buy the farm."

"SAM! SAM!" called Miller. He flew escape maneuvers. Three surface-to-air missiles flew past the Apache.

"They ain't got my name on 'em," announced Buddy, squeezing off the cannon to prove that he had *their* names. The three mobile SAM vehicles went up in fire and smoke.

"Damn, Velasco, we got more targets than we can shoot at!" cried Riggs.

"No, I gonna do it all, man. I gonna do it all with our conrades in arms," returned Velasco.

The three Apaches attacked as one, blasting everything they got in their sights.

Pytor Kolchak stood behind the waist-high berm and directed his men to keep firing at the two attacking helicopters. The Cossack didn't fear any mortal man, not even man's machines. He had lived too many years by his wits and he was going to die by them.

The attack helicopters were effective. They were devastatingly effective, and he was losing his armor and missile protection. It angered him that his men weren't better shots.

An Apache dove to make a run at the position where Pytor was standing. He yelled, "Fire straight, you fools! Fire to kill!"

Pytor kicked his radio operator and jumped up on the berm with his pistol drawn. He aimed it and carefully squeezed the trigger, one well-directed shot after another. A 30mm cannon round caught him high in the left chest and blew his shoulder and arm off. The exploding round opened his ribcage and tore out his dirty, evil heart, blasting it into a thousand pieces and scattering it across the ground. The meat would feed the vultures, the only creatures with stomachs that could process such evil.

Buddy saw it coming. It was a SAM with friends close behind. "SAM! SAM!"

"Got 'em!" called Miller.

Miller pulled the nose of the apache up and fell off to the right. The SAM passed by, close, but it was a miss. Three other SAMs followed the first one. He pulled the Apache back into line, and it ran into a 125mm round fired from a T-72 tank. The round passed through the bottom of the fuselage and exploded to the rear of the engines. The explosion took off the tail section of the Apache and two of the rotor blades.

Miller had time to yell, "We're hit! We're hit!" before the helicopter reached to the ground. It exploded on impact.

Truck was listening to the radio transmission when he heard Miller's last call. He read off the location of Red Dog's Apache and turned to fly to his location. "What ya got, Dog?"

"Don't fly into this area. It's too hot for that Hawk."

"We're on our way, boss. Stand aside and let us take this on," Bad Bear called over the air.

Truck growled. That was all he could do. His helicopter was hardened more than the old UH-1, but it still had too many exposed areas that could be easily damaged by small rounds such as the 23mm.

Red Dog and Crackers flew with anger in their hearts and killing on their minds. They had just returned from the forward base with a full load of ordnance.

Horwitz and Pylant began a systematic cleanup of the tanks and SAMs left on site. Red Dog and Riggs joined them until they were out of ordnance and had to return to resupply their Apache.

"We'll be back. Save me some of those fuckers," called Red Dog as he and Riggs flew off.

"Not if I can help it," mumbled Crackers.

Tanks and mobile SAMs started backing off and tried to find cover from the unrelenting machines in the sky.

On call, a flight of Russian helicopters flew into the area and unloaded its troops.

Truck came into the area to assess the damage to the downed Apache. Parts were scattered over the hillside, but he had to make sure that there was no classified equipment the Russians or Azerbaidzhan governments could get their hands on. "I'm going down. Ride shotgun."

"That's a roger, boss," said Bad Bear.

The Blackhawk landed. Truck left the helicopter running and he and Hunter went to inspect the crash site. The two crewmen jumped out of the aircraft with their rifles and took positions to guard the area.

There were very few large pieces of the helicopter's instrument panel left intact. Body parts of the two crewmen were also found.

Hunter picked up a few classified items and took them back to the Blackhawk.

Truck returned to the helicopter and called over the air, "White Boy! White Boy! This is Blue Dad. Do you read me? Over!"

After a moment, Willie's voice replied, "I read you loud and clear. Over."

"Check with your counterpart and see if he will let you bring some men for a cleanup detail at this location. Over."

"Will do, Blue Dad. Out!"

Willie looked at Klemens. Klemens had heard the transmission. He had heard the radio call from the Americans as they were going down and knew of their crash. "We will help. I will get you people."

"Thanks, Colonel," replied Willie.

"They gave you call sign of White Boy?" asked Klemens with a grin.

"Yeah. Them friends of mine think it's a blast to call me white boy," Willie answered with a chuckle. "But the laugh's on them. I be anything I want."

Klemens assigned two Mi-17 Hips and men to assist him.

The crash site was a mess. It was difficult to police up the area with a war going on around them. But Truck was not going to leave his men or his aircraft behind.

The Russians gave the Americans the use of an Mi-26 Halo to transport the remains of Miller and Buddy back to the rear airfield along with what was left of the Apache.

The battle was over for the Americans. The Polish commandos had also completed their mission. The Poles were loaded on helicopters and flown back to the Russian border where they were to load onto their aircraft and return to Poland. The sooner the Poles got out of Russian territory the better the Russians liked it. The Russians had nothing over the Poles, who had just as much animosity toward their former rulers.

The Azerbaidzhan Army had not appeared during the battle on their own territory. They had stood aside and allowed the Russians to clean up the mess as they had agreed. When the fight was over, they went to the battle-field and demanded that the Russians leave their territory. They had international law on their side on that issue.

Daglarie shook hands with the men from the House of Omet. He had been among warriors and it made him feel good. When he shook hands with Fezi, the older Azerbaidzhan warrior kissed him on both cheeks before he stepped back. Ata also bid Daglarie goodbye. Faruk, Kemal's eldest son, arrived and presented him with two bejeweled daggers. One was for himself and the other was for Selma.

"Tell your father that I will return for a visit," said Daglarie.

"It is expected and hoped for," said Faruk. "And also bring that moon-eyed comrade with you."

The men laughed. Selma had been so obvious that the entire family knew of his admiration for the beautiful Mubeccel.

The Hind flew in and landed. An American SF trooper

got out of the helicopter, stood beside the door and waited for Daglarie.

The American waved one last time and ran to the helicopter. He got in without looking back.

The Russians were still fighting in the mountains.

23

"Okay, Dot, I'll try to get up to Bragg in a few days," Truck told her and put the phone down in its cradle. He wanted to see Dot Botts worse than he liked to admit. When he was least expecting it, a picture of those large, soft breasts came to mind and threw him off what he was supposed to be doing. Her looks and lovemaking were not the only things he liked about her—by God, he liked her company. She had just been informed that she was going to be appointed a brigadier general. Her first act was to call him and tell him the good news before she called her family or anyone else. He wondered what it was going to be like to be married to a general. He thought he could handle it.

Truck left his desk and walked into the outer office. He looked at Crackers and said, "Get the men together."

"On the way, boss," replied Crackers, who left immediately to call a formation.

* * *

The men filed into the area of the hangar where their formations were held. They stood together in the teams to which they were assigned. Donald Day, the old air force observation pilot, stood to one side, alone, the way he flew most of the time, and waited. The men talked among themselves, since this was one of the few times they paused long enough from their work to just visit. The black warbirds were prominent features in the background, their sinister-looking weapons at rest. Even sitting quietly, the powerful machines looked as if they were ready to jump into action on a moment's notice.

The men had gotten their equipment in order and new parts ordered as soon as the team returned from Azerbaidzhan. Repairs were made, and most of the equipment was already combat ready. After a complete inspection of Crackers's damaged helicopter, it was determined that the frame was damaged, so the entire machine had to be replaced. Two new Apaches were requisitioned to replace the ones lost in combat. Things were getting to be ship-shape, and it was about time the men relaxed. There were other things in the world other than helicopters, weapons and thoughts of war. None of the men knew much about anything else, but they had families who told them to pay attention to non-military matters.

Truck walked out in front of the formation. He stood a moment, waiting to get the men's full attention. It didn't take long. Then he looked the team over with his one good eye.

"I just got a report that Hernandez's arm will be saved, but his flying days are over," Truck told them. "Wild Bill had some reconstruction work on his legs and back, and a new joint was placed in his hip. Plus, he's got three cracked vertebrae and nearly every disc in his backbone is bruised. He will not come back to the team.''

There were groans in the ranks when the men heard the conditions of their two friends.

''We're fortunate to have the guy who is chief of orthopedics down at Brooke Army Hospital on our side. He works for all the U.S. Army special operations groups and us kind of guys are his interest,'' Truck told them.

Heads nodded in appreciation that someone was looking out for them.

''We went, we saw and we conquered. That's the way we always do it. The Red Russians were no different from anyone else we've faced, and they bit the dust under our might,'' Truck said. ''It took a few days for the Russians to clean up their little battlefield, but we did our job before we left. And the world is safer for what we did.

''I got a call from Bragg, and all men who were flying and involved in ground operations will be awarded the Legion of Merit. All other men will receive the Joint Service Commendation Medal. The decorations will be placed in your files and you might get them someday. That's all they can give us, since we're not at war with anyone—so we can't get combat decorations.'' Truck paused. He continued, ''And I'm gonna get all of you two weeks off to be with your families. And it won't count against your leave time. This is a little in-country R and R, sponsored by yours truly and the big bosses.''

The men cheered.

''We're also getting some extra contingency money so you guys can get a big bonus for such a good job. Of course, you always do a good job. You're among the best soldiers I've ever served with, and I've been around a while. I salute you.''

Truck turned and went back into his office.

The men started yelling their appreciation for the time off and the extra money. That was a lot better than any decoration.

Crackers had to stand on a table and yell above the noise to get the men's attention. When they finally quieted down, he said, "Tomorrow morning there will be memorial services for Wild Bill and Buddy."

That information brought a sobering quiet to the men.

"I don't reckon we have to tell everyone to be there," he said. "I think we've been a lucky bunch of sonsabitches to have a man like that old one-eyed bastard to lead us. I'll never forget him, this bunch and what we've done. There's never been a group to match this one, and there won't ever be.

"Dismissed."

The formation broke up.

Bad Bear and Red Dog walked into Truck's office carrying mugs of coffee. Willie and Stu joined them, and Donald Day joined them a bit later. All of the old hands, the "old men" of the team, were present.

"Where do we go from here?" asked Stu.

The others shrugged their shoulders.

"I don't know where, but if asked, we'll go," said Day.

"I'm already ready," was Bad Bear's only comment. The Kiowa was a warrior from a warrior people. He didn't know what he was going to do, but he sure wasn't going to sit quietly on his ass. He knew that he and Truck would come up with something exciting if the team was ever demobilized.

The men stood a moment, thinking about the future of their profession.

"Do ya know, boys, we're running out of wars to fight," Truck announced.

Silence fell over the men. It was a dark, thick silence that covered them like a blanket and left them depressed. The prospect of no battles for the remainder of their lifetimes left them without a reason for living. They felt like sailors with all the oceans dried up and all the ships scrapped or dry docked.

"Man, this is worse than a cowboy without a horse," put in Stu.

The men nodded their heads in sorrow.

"I can't see myself tied down to no one spot, running to the store an' doin' make-work just to keep from crying," Willie said.

"I agree with that," said Day. He looked at them and said in a firm voice, "And, no, I ain't gonna crawl back into a bottle. I've enjoyed being sober too much."

The men got quiet and stood, looking at the floor or walls or at their mugs of coffee. They looked everywhere but at each other.

"I think I'm gonna get drunk," said Truck, and he walked out of the room.

The men followed.

Cadet Coy Vestal leaned against the wall and stared out the window of his room. From the fourth floor, he had a clear view of the Hudson River, dark and swift from the spring rains, as it surged past its verdant banks. Unusually warm weather had forced the trees to bud and bloom ahead of time, producing a profusion of color on the normally drab landscape.

Vestal watched as the graduating cadets' relatives mixed with alumni and visiting dignitaries on their way to the reviewing stands.

He had less than an hour before he would join the formation and graduate from West Point, less than an hour before he would to be a brand new second lieutenant, the first in his military family to graduate from the Academy, the first to be a commissioned officer.

His roommate was already out there with the other graduates. They were all looking forward to what would be one of the happiest days of their lives, a moment of achievement, the great beginning for which they had labored. Vestal stared out the window, waiting for some feeling of euphoria to sweep over him.

He didn't feel the joy, the excitement, the sense of achievement. He was feeling his stomach tighten from the slow constriction of his own internal pressures.

Turning from the window, he glanced across the room at the packed boxes and footlockers awaiting shipment. Everything he owned was in these boxes, neatly packed. All his uniforms, boots, books—everything he looked to for answers was contained in the crates. He realized, as he looked over it all, how very little there was. Like the packed belongings, he was now an alien in the stark little room. He could no longer find refuge here; like these boxes, he was awaiting transport to a new location.

No doubt the uniforms, all expensively tailored and made of the finest materials, would be perfect for their call to duty, but, Vestal thought as his stomach knotted, was he?

Would the uniforms, so perfect in every detail, cover up the man inside, the man who desperately wished he wasn't leaving West Point, the man who would now be called on to perform?

He absentmindedly straightened his tunic, running his fingers over the woolen fabric. These were the last moments of privacy for the day; shortly he would become one more in a "long gray line," one more piece of the great tradition of the United States Military Academy.

As he nervously clenched and unclenched his fist, he studied the class ring on his finger. It seemed heavy, a colossal weight, as if it contained all the responsibilities and duties expected of him.

He wished his father were there. He needed a chance to talk to him, to ask him if he had ever been afraid, if he had ever felt unsure, if he had ever felt confusion. But those were questions that could never be answered. His father was long gone, a hero, fallen on the field of honor in Southeast Asia. His death and posthumous Medal of Honor had been Vestal's ticket to West Point.

Perhaps his uncles, all Airborne, all retired now as sergeants major, could answer those questions, but Vestal knew he wouldn't ask them. They were out there now with his mother, waiting anxiously to see him graduate.

He couldn't possibly admit fear, confusion, his unsure concept of himself to them. He was John Vestal's only child, his son, and the last fragment they had of their heroic brother. He couldn't let them know how he was feeling now. He didn't have the right to spoil their illusion of who he was. And right now, that was all he really was—an illusion of a strong military man, a new officer, a man who knew where he was going, what he was made of, and who would lead men into battle. He shook in his shoes, looking back out the window as the door swung open.

"Hey, Coy! Your uncles are downstairs waiting. They want to walk over to formation with you."

Vestal, yanked abruptly from his thoughts, turned to face Vince Caruso. His roommate was flushed with excitement as he stood nervously in the door.

"I'm on my way down. You ready for your big 'moment of truth'?" Vestal said, forcing a smile.

"That's affirmative! I am ready to shed this place and get on with it." Caruso answered, looking at his watch. "We better get a move on."

"Hey," Vestal reached over to pick up his hat. "I wasn't talking about graduation. You're getting married tomorrow, remember? That's the 'moment of truth,' when your beautiful fiancée finds out how bad your breath is in the morning!"

"Man," Caruso strutted in the doorway, smoothing his

tunic, "she's so dazzled by my manliness, she'll never notice. I gotta go, she's waiting for me. Don't forget to bring your mother to the rehearsal dinner tonight."

Vestal nodded and waved as his roommate charged off down the hall. He walked into the hallway, took one last glance into the room, then closed the door behind him. It was time for the "illusion" to perform, time to close all doors behind him and face whatever stood before him.

George Patton "Jeep" Laliker waited in front of the building, feeling as conspicuous and uncomfortable as the bastard child at a family reunion.

One thing was for sure, his Texas A&M uniform—the traditional Eisenhower jacket, with the Sam Browne belt over the gray-pink jodhpurs and highly polished brown riding boots—stood out. He reached up and adjusted his campaign hat, worn with this uniform only on auspicious occasions, and tried to ignore the stares of the people passing by.

Glancing down at his watch for the fifth time in fifteen minutes, Jeep sighed and shifted nervously from one foot to the other.

The two stars on his shoulder designated his position in the Corps at A&M, Cadet Lieutenant Colonel, the highest rank possible, first in his graduating class. That position had earned him a Regular Army commission upon graduation, in a day when many of the graduates were being released to the reserves to serve their commitments. Jeep was proud of his position, proud of his high standing at A&M, but here at West Point, alma mater of past generations of the Laliker family, he was experiencing a recurring sense of failure.

This was where he had thought he would be. He had dreamed and planned since he was a child of standing here today, waiting to graduate from the Academy. He had done everything necessary to become accepted—the high grade average, the leadership positions in the high school programs, participation in sports. West Point looked for the complete individual, well rounded and excelling in all areas. Jeep was a contender.

The sports had been his downfall. To become captain of his high school football team, he had taken one too many chances on the field, played with everything in him, and broken his leg in the last season. The break and subsequent lengthy healing period had cost him his slot of first alternate to the U.S. Military Academy. It had been a bitter disappointment, one that rose up in his mind and haunted him still.

Even though his family had played down his loss, encouraging him to take the scholarship to Texas A&M, he knew he was the only male member of his family, since the establishment of the Military Academy, to not attend. Admitting defeat was also not a family trait, and Jeep had hidden his disappointment, working hard to recover from the broken leg and pushing himself to the limit at A&M. He never discussed his missed opportunity at the Academy and overachieved to fill his personal void.

His father had graduated high in his class, gone into the infantry, earned his Airborne wings and served two tours in Vietnam with the 101st. On his second tour his APC had hit a land mine and he'd lost one arm and both legs. Even though he had retired from the military on a medical discharge, he kept close contact with his fellow graduates, never missing a graduation.

In years past, Mrs. Laliker had attended the ceremonies with her husband, helping him maneuver around the campus in his wheelchair, but this year Jeep's grandmother had been hospitalized the week before graduation, forcing his mother to stay behind. When she called and asked Jeep to attend, she hadn't realized the effect it would have on her son.

So here he stood, anguishing instead of celebrating. This was Senior Week back at College Station. There, he'd be going out to parties, accepting all the honor and respect he'd gained as Cadet Lieutenant Colonel. Instead, he was standing on the campus of the school he hadn't measured up to, waiting to watch graduate the men and women who would always have date-of-rank on him by one week, while his father visited with old friends in the building behind him.

To pass the time, he watched the passersby as they congregated in little groups around the walkway, waiting for the graduation parade to start. He glanced down at his watch again and was pleased to see it was nearing time for him to go back inside for his father. He turned and walked past three sergeants major standing in their uniforms by the door. He bounded up the stairs, swung open the door and collided with a cadet in the doorway, knocking the man off balance. The cadet's hat fell and rolled out on the step.

"Whoa!" Laliker said, stepping back to steady himself.

"Hey!" the startled Cadet yelled, watching as the man in front of him backed up. "Watch it! You're standing on my hat!"

Laliker looked down. Sure enough, he had planted one of his boots squarely on the brim of the cadet's hat. As he reached down to retrieve it, they bumped heads, knocking Laliker back a step. Before Jeep could apologize, the angry cadet yanked the hat from the ground, muttering under his breath, and took a long look at the offender.

As he nervously wiped at the scrape on the highly polished brim, he looked up Laliker.

"You clumsy bastard!" A twisted smile formed on his lips as he recognized the A&M uniform. "What are you dressed up for?" he asked. "A costume ball? Looks like you wore the wrong costume for his party, 'Second-stringer.' "

Laliker, incensed by the insult, squared his jaw and stepped forward. "Look, you arrogant asshole, I—"

"Gentlemen!" A voice barked out from behind them.

They both turned to see who was speaking. A gray-haired major, who bore a striking resemblance to the A&M cadet, scowled at them both from his wheelchair. The West Point cadet came to attention and saluted as Laliker stepped past him and stood behind the chair.

"Sir," the cadet stammered, pushing the door open, "allow me."

Major Laliker returned the salute and nodded as Jeep, eyes blazing, pushed the wheelchair past and down the ramp.

The cadet hurriedly joined some older men and rushed past the Lalikers to the formation. Jeep watched, still stinging from his slur, as he pushed his father toward the reviewing stands in silence. After the chair had been placed on the stand, Jeep walked around and stood beside his dad.

Major Laliker had been glancing through the program, giving his son time to cool down. He cleared his throat. "You want to talk about that?" he said, looking up at Jeep.

"No, I expected it!" Jeep said angrily.

The major shifted uncomfortably in the chair. "Get the chip off your shoulder, son. It doesn't become you. He didn't mean what he said."

"The hell he didn't!"

"Look," Major Laliker said, as the band struck the first chords of a march and the parade began, "he's strung tight today; so are you. Just write it off to nerves. I saw his name tag and looked him up. That's John Vestal's son. He's probably a good man."

"Vestal?" Jeep questioned, looking down at his father. "He graduated with you?"

"No. John Vestal was a master sergeant and died in Viet-Nam. He was awarded the Medal of Honor."

"Just because his dad died to get him into the academy, doesn't mean he's a 'good man.'"

"Well, you could be right. At any rate, you'll have the opportunity to find out soon enough. You're both headed in the same direction," Major Laliker said, looking out over the cadets as they marched by. "The program has the destination of each cadet next to his name. Just like you, Coy Vestal is headed for Ranger School and the 82nd Airborne Division."